THE COTTON MILL ORPHAN

Victorian Romance

FAYE GODWIN

Tica House
Publishing

Sweet Romance that Delights and Enchants!

PERSONAL WORD FROM THE AUTHOR

DEAREST READERS,

I'm so delighted that you have chosen one of my books to read. I am proud to be a part of the team of writers at Tica House Publishing. Our goal is to inspire, entertain, and give you many hours of reading pleasure. Your kind words and loving readership are deeply appreciated.

I would like to personally invite you to sign up for updates and to become part of our **Exclusive Reader Club**—it's completely Free to Join! I'd love to welcome you!

Much love,

Faye Godwin

CLICK HERE to Join our Reader's Club and to Receive Tica House Updates!

https://victorian.subscribemenow.com/

CONTENTS

PART I

CHAPTER 1

JULIETTE PURCELL COULDN'T STOP THINKING of the piece of bread in the wooden crate.

She sat cross-legged on the sleeping pallet, trying her best to focus on gazing out of the window, or rather, out of the single windowpane that still had any glass in it. The big square window once had four panes. Now only one remained, small and grimy; the other three were boarded up, with cardboard stuffed into the cracks between the bits of rotten wood and the rusted edges of the window frame.

Still, it offered more than most of the little tenements inside this building had: a view of the outside world. Sleet drummed quietly against the glass, but Juliette could still make out the muffled figures moving along the street below. It was a fairly busy thoroughfare, churned into mud by the constant passage of tired feet. Now, as usual, most of the traffic was pedestrian. Men and women in grey and black garments, their heads tucked low, the lucky ones clinging to scrubby umbrellas with frayed edges, hurried to and fro on whatever hidden mission grownups always seemed to have. There were a few bony, toothless old men huddled against the bottom of the opposite building, curled up on beds of old newspapers, with bits of cardboard spread over them to protect them from the rain. Now and then one of them extended a skeletal hand toward the crowd. The hand was almost always completely ignored.

Juliette watched the thin men and wondered why they didn't have any homes to go to. She watched the sleet and thought of the coming winter, when there would be snow, and slush, and bitter cold, and her mother would complain almost constantly of the price of coal.

She tried to think of anything—*anything*—except the piece of bread in the wooden crate. Still, her eyes dragged slowly across the tenement room. It was tiny, little more than a corner of the building, holding only the pallet, a fireplace, and the crate. The crate in which her mother always put whatever food she could find and hide for supper.

She'd put something in there this morning when she'd returned briefly from the Thompson home and headed to the Barnaby's to do their washing. It was all Mama ever did— scrub other people's dirty clothes, until her hands were red and chapped with the work.

The bread was for supper, Juliette knew. But the last time she'd eaten was supper the night before, and it felt like an awfully long time ago.

"Juliette," said Reuben, "what did Mama put in the box this morning?"

Juliette looked down at her little brother. He lay curled up with his head in her lap, and his big brown eyes gazed up at her, filled with a silent plea. He was as hungry as she was, Juliette knew. His bony shoulder jutted into her bony leg, but she didn't complain. She just ran her hands through his greasy blond curls.

"Money, I think," she lied.

Reuben sighed. "Let's take it. Buy food."

"Mama will bring food when she comes home," Juliette promised, praying that the crust of bread wasn't all they had for supper for the three of them.

Reuben scowled. "She'll give money to the man."

Juliette knew instantly which man he was talking about: a stooped, scowling, sallow-faced creature who came around every Monday and took money from everyone who lived in the building. It was a Monday, she realized painfully. That bread *was* all they had.

"Maybe," she said weakly.

"We buy food." Reuben sat up.

"Roo, no," said Juliette. "We have to be patient. Mama will feed us."

"Food," Reuben insisted, walking toward the crate.

Juliette grabbed his arm. "Stop."

It was then that she heard it: a faint, hissing sound in the hallway outside their tenement. She felt the nervousness drain from her belly and grinned. "Wait, Roo, do you hear that?"

Reuben's little face lit up. "Margie," he cried.

Together, the children raced out of the scrap of ragged linen that served as a door. They stepped into a narrow hallway, barely wide enough to admit a broad-shouldered man. On either side of the hallway, makeshift doors led into tenements as tiny and pitiful as their own. The walls weren't straight; they wandered, jutting out in places, retreating in others. Some of the doors were wooden. Others were scraps of fabric or cardboard. Some were simply missing.

The hissing sound came from a broom made from a bundle of twigs, lashed to an old bit of wood with a piece of dirty string. It was wielded by a bony woman with huge green eyes and a blue dress, faded to sickly grey, that hung shapelessly from her unsubstantial frame.

"Margie," Reuben squealed and ran across the floor to her.

Margie leaned the broom against a wall—it shuddered; it was only made of planks—and wrapped her arms around Reuben when he hugged her thighs. Juliette followed a little more slowly, but still hugged Margie's waist. Unlike almost everything else in this building, the woman smelled of cheap soap.

"Children, children," Margie chuckled. "It's good to see you."

"You bring us something?" Reuben asked, gazing up at her adoringly.

Margie's eyes danced. "Of course, I did." She reached into the threadbare pocket of her apron and drew out a single, cold, boiled potato. It was cut in half, and she gave half to Reuben, half to Juliette.

The children gulped down the scrap of food so quickly that it hardly seemed to have ever existed. Still, its cold presence in the pit of Juliette's stomach was better than nothing.

"What do we say, Roo?" she reminded her brother.

Reuben clutched Margie's hand. "Thank you, Margie."

"Thank you, Margie," Juliette echoed.

Margie laughed. "Of course, my little ones. Now, have you come to help me clean the building today?"

Juliette and Reuben nodded earnestly, and Margie smiled. She picked up the holey metal pail she always carried around with her; its companion was only slightly less holey, and still leaked cold water onto the wooden floor.

"Come on, then." she said cheerfully. "I'll sweep, you two can scrub."

She doled out a scrubbing brush to each of them—half a scrubbing brush, to be precise; it had fortuitously split down the middle one day when Reuben and Juliette were arguing over it—and they set to work. Margie went down the hall with the broom first, sweeping away the dust and mud, knocking the cobwebs from the corners. The children followed on their hands and knees, scrubbing the splintery floor as well as they could with nothing but cold water to wash away the dirt.

There were many hallways in the tenement building, and Margie was the only person who ever tried to clean them all. This one was particularly dirty today, after the rain had turned the street into mud over the past week. Juliette gritted her teeth and scrubbed with both hands, working the clumps of dirt loose. Reuben was more half-hearted, but he still knocked away some of the mud.

"Harder, Roo," Juliette ordered him.

"My arms get tired," Reuben complained.

"Then go back inside," said Juliette.

He shook his head, round-eyed. "No. I'm helping."

"And you're doing a wonderful job, too, little Roo," said Margie cheerfully.

Reuben grinned, his face lighting up, and he set to work with an even better will than before.

Margie always hummed while she swept, and it was one of the reasons why Juliette so loved helping her. Her mother never sang or hummed; she only came home from work, fell down on the pallet, and slept. But Margie hummed often and burst into song regularly, and her soft, high voice was a thread of beauty in Juliette's desperate life.

They cleaned the entire hallway, and Juliette had almost succeeded in forgetting her hunger when she and Margie scrubbed out the last corners. Reuben had bored of the work —he was only four, after all—and sat watching on an upturned bucket.

"There," said Margie. She straightened up. "Isn't that so much better?"

They looked back along the hallway. It was still very crooked, and the smell of unwashed humanity still oozed from the rooms that lined it. But Margie was right. Being able to see the wooden floor, and having all the cobwebs gone from the corners, made it seem a little more tolerable.

"It looks grand," said Reuben.

"Grand." Margie chuckled. "I hardly think so." She straight-ened some more, winced, and clutched at her chest.

Juliette grabbed her arm. "Margie?" she gasped.

"I'm all right, pet." Margie let out a breath, but it made a rattling sound in her chest. "I just... I need a little rest, that's all."

Reuben jumped off the upturned bucket and hurried to bring it over, and Margie sat down sharply, leaning against the wall. Her lips were ringed with a bluish tinge, and what little colour remained in her pinched face had vanished.

Juliette hated Margie's breathless spells. She clutched her friend's cold hand tightly, and Reuben snuggled into her lap. Margie leaned her head back against the wall and wrapped her free arm around Reuben where he perched on her bony thighs.

"Margie?" Reuben whispered, when Margie's breathing had begun to slow.

"Yes, poppet?" said Margie.

"Why do you clean the hallway?" Reuben asked, raising his head.

Margie smiled. "No one else does."

"But why do *you*?" asked Juliette.

Margie took another two rattling breaths. "Cleaning our home cleans our hearts." She smiled. "My mama always used to say that to me. We had a beautiful, clean house."

"The one in the country that you tell us about?" asked Juliette.

"Yes, poppet, the very same," said Margie.

"The one with all the animals." Reuben giggled. "Piggies and puppies and lambies."

"And cows and goats and chickens," said Margie.

"Don't forget the chickens." Reuben grinned.

Juliette leaned her head against Margie's arm. It was a little warmer now. "Will you take us there someday?"

"Oh, poppet." Margie wrapped her arm around Juliette. "I hope I can. One day."

❦

JULIETTE SAT CURLED by the window, her small hands shaking. Her stomach felt so empty that she imagined it being shrivelled up, like the old dry orange peel lying in the street below, curled and blasted by the wind. Juliette wondered if you could eat orange peels the way you could eat apple cores if you rinsed them in the gutter first.

She watched as the front door of the tenement building swung open. Their mother, Beatrice, stepped outside. She was bent and withered by the wind even before she closed the door behind her, her headscarf rippling as the savage wind tore at it. Beatrice shuffled a few steps along the street, then stopped to stare up at the window. Dutifully, Juliette and Reuben both smiled and waved. Beatrice's pinched, reddened face creased in a returning smile, and she waved back.

Both children waited until their mother was completely lost in the crowd of workers flowing down the street, bare flesh flashing where their torn trousers and ruined shoes exposed their skin to the biting cold. Then Reuben jumped to his feet.

"Come on." He grabbed Juliette's hand. "Let's go."

Juliette hesitated. "I don't know, Roo," she said. "Maybe we'll be all right until supper."

Reuben's little face crumpled. "Juli... I'm so hungry."

"I know you are." Juliette had been right about supper last night. Beatrice had given all of her money to the sallow-faced man, and the crust of bread in the crate had been all they had. Beatrice had promised that she wasn't hungry, but Juliette had seen the way her eyes bored into the bread that she and Reuben devoured. She wanted to be grateful that their mother had given them everything she had, but the bread had hardly seemed to touch her stomach before it was all gone.

"Please, Juli." Reuben's eyes filled with tears.

"It's just that Mama hates it when we go outside," said Juliette. "You know she does. She's so afraid someone will take us."

Reuben sobbed. "But I'm *hungry*."

Juliette was hungry too, so, so hungry, and she couldn't bear her poor baby brother's weeping. She reached out and wrapped her hand around his. "All right," she said. "Let's go."

They shuffled down the spotless hallway, and Juliette hesitated when they reached one of the few wooden doors on this third floor of the building. It had been neatly sanded, if not painted, and the number—15—had been drawn on it in charcoal.

"Maybe Margie has something for us to eat," she whispered.

Reuben looked up at her with big eyes. Juliette reached out and knocked gently. "Margie?" she called.

Bert, Margie's husband, would have left for the docks even before Beatrice went to work. But Margie was always home.

"Margie," Juliette whispered and pushed the door open a little wider.

The tenement was completely spotless. It, too, sported a single window; the glass was perfectly clean, and there were no cobwebs in the corners. The floor was neatly swept, even though all it contained was a mat for eating, a sleeping pallet, and a suitcase with scuffed corners.

Margie lay curled on the sleeping pallet, fast asleep, her arms wrapped around her flat belly. Her breath was slow and easy, but Juliette knew that Bert must have given her some of the medicine that made her sleep. She'd be no help today.

With a heavy heart, Juliette closed the door and led Reuben down the rickety, squeaking steps. They had to cross the ground floor to reach the front door, and here many of the tenants were very, very old. They mostly had curtains instead of doors, and where the curtains were pulled back, old folk hunkered in their own waste stared as the children went past. Their yellow eyes were like clawing fingers, trying to pull Juliette back.

She kept her eyes on the front door and forcefully pulled Reuben outside into the bitter wind. The street was bleak and busy; pedestrians flooded the muddy road, ignoring the single donkey cart that laboured up the street, peddling rags and bones. Stray dogs argued over a dead rat on the corner, and Juliette tried not to stare at the homeless men that muttered and oozed in the shadows of the building across the road.

She kept a firm grip on Reuben's hand as they joined the flood of pedestrians, following them down the block to the market square at the end of the street. Here, at least, the ground was covered in uneven cobblestones. A little church reared its modest spire over the ramshackle roofs that surrounded the square, and there were brick-and-mortar shops as well as the rickety stalls composed of sticks and rags where old women sold bone broth and skinny men repaired shoes that should have been re-soled long ago.

Juliette was grateful to see that their usual corner was empty. She led Reuben to the spot under a wrought-iron streetlight and kept a hand clenched firmly around his. A chill crept down her spine, and she turned around quickly to stare into the mouth of the dark alleyway behind them. It had felt as though something had been watching her, but the alleyway was empty. Juliette breathed a sigh of relief and turned her attention back to the crowd.

The crowds here were slightly more well-heeled than they were just a block away, in front of the tenement building. Most of the people here had patches instead of rips in their clothes; their toes weren't showing, and they had pink cheeks and baskets on their arms for shopping.

"Alms?" Juliette called, holding out her thin hand. "Any alms for the poor?"

She looked hopefully at a plump woman who hurried by with a shopping basket filled with bread and carrots and cheeses and fish, but the woman didn't spare her a glance.

"Oh, please, sir." Reuben fell to his knees and extended his small hands. "Any alms for a hungry child?"

An elderly gentleman with a walking stick stopped and gazed down at Reuben. The little boy's eyes were huge and sorrowful, and his golden mop of hair tumbled over them.

"Sorry state the world's in," the gentleman mumbled. He dug in his pocket and tossed a penny into Reuben's hands.

The boy closed his hands delightedly and turned to Juliette as the gentleman left. "Juli. Can we go and get bread now?"

"Not yet," Juliette told him. "Almost. Almost."

Reuben sighed and settled onto his knees again.

They were extending their arms to the crowd once more when a cheerful voice spoke behind Juliette. "Hello, hello, Juli and Roo. How lovely to see the pair of you."

Juliette laughed at the rhyme and spun around. A grinning boy stood on the sidewalk behind her, clutching the tatty satchel that he always carried with him. His hair had been shaven off for lice last year, and it was still short and tufty, sticking out in places through his threadbare tweed cap. He wore a jaunty smile cocked at the same angle as his cap.

"Emory," said Juliette. "Hello."

"Someone gave me a penny," said Reuben, proudly displaying it.

"Now that's good news, lad," said Emory happily. He could call Reuben "lad" because he was a big boy already; eleven years old, three years Juliette's senior. "Hopefully you'll get much more."

"What about you?" Juliette asked. "How are you?"

"Fair-to-middling," said Emory. "Sold a few trinkets, looking for a few more." He opened the satchel and showed Juliette the things he fished out of gutters or garbage heaps and cleaned up in an attempt to sell them for a few ha'pennies: bits of broken glass, scraps of old newspaper, rags and bones.

"Uncle Joe needs help making the rent this week. Hopefully we'll have money left for bread and cheese."

"I hope so, too, for your part," said Juliette.

"It won't do to complain, will it?" said Emory brightly.

"Oh, Emory," said Reuben, "tell us a story."

A spindly girl on doe-like legs paused to drop a ha'penny into Reuben's hands, and he closed them quickly, then gave Emory a pleading look.

"I don't know if I have time for a story," said Emory.

"Just a small one," said Juliette. "Please."

Emory's crooked smile returned. "Oh, all right," he said. "I suppose I have time for a little one."

"Hooray." Reuben clapped his small hands, his smile so endearing that another young lady stopped and tossed him a penny.

Reuben had just tucked the penny away when Emory began, leaning against a lamppost. "Once upon a time," he said, "there were three little rabbits."

"Hares, or rabbits?" asked Reuben.

"Rabbits, Roo," said Juliette crossly. "Listen to the story."

"Rabbits, indeed," said Emory. "Two little brown ones and a little grey one. The grey one was a bit bigger, and one of the brown ones was a little smaller." His eyes met Juliette's. "The brown one in the middle was just right."

Juliette smiled. She could tell the middle one was Emory's favorite.

"The three little rabbits lived in a marsh," said Emory.

"A nice marsh?" Reuben asked.

Emory shook his head. "A nasty marsh, honestly. It often smelled bad, and a lot of the rabbits got sick."

"The poor rabbits," sighed Juliette.

"Some people used to tell the rabbits that they would never escape the marsh," Emory went on. "They said that they would spend the rest of their lives there. But the big grey rabbit would never believe them. He always thought there must be a nicer place to live, somewhere they could kick up their heels and dig nice warrens that never got all damp and horrible with mud."

"All rabbits should have that," said Reuben.

"I think so, too," said Emory.

"What happened to them?" Juliette asked. "Did they ever find a way out of the marsh?"

Emory met her eyes, and his smile was smaller now, but it warmed her down to the marrow of her bones.

"Yes," he said. "Yes, I think they did."

CHAPTER 2

THE WIND WAS FIERCELY cold now, nipping cruelly at Juliette's exposed ears. She brushed at her grimy hair, trying to use it to cover them.

"Come *on*, Roo," she said. "We need to hurry up if we're going to get home before Mama does."

Reuben's mouth drooped at the corners. "My feet are tired," he complained.

Juliette grabbed his hand and tugged him forward. "I know, but Mama will be so angry if she finds out where we've been."

She couldn't understand why Reuben was whining. They'd made enough money, thanks to his soulful eyes and sweet voice, that they'd been able to buy half a loaf of bread in the market about an hour ago. Both children had eaten their fill.

Juliette relished the feeling of having a full stomach, even if they'd only washed the bread down with cups of grimy water from the pump in the middle of the market.

"I want to sleep," Reuben moaned.

"Then hurry up so that we can get home and you can sleep," Juliette snapped.

The little boy screwed his free fist into his eye socket and rubbed his eye hard. Juliette sighed. He was only four, she reminded himself, although it was difficult not to recognize in the same breath that she was only eight herself.

"Come on, Roo," she said. "We'll be home soon."

A few minutes later, they were climbing the rickety stairwell, and Juliette couldn't help noticing the cobwebs and dust in all the corners of the stairs. She felt a pang of worry and wondered when Margie would be back to herself again.

As they reached the second floor landing, Juliette glanced out of the window, and immediately spotted her. Even though there was a crowd of people shuffling along the streets now in the evening gloom, a heavy grey mist hanging over the street, she still picked out her mother at first glance. Beatrice's head hung, as always, covered in a tattered and faded floral bonnet. She moved slowly, her shoulders very slumped.

"Roo, hurry!" Juliette gasped.

She tugged Reuben along after her and they scampered up the last flight of steps together, then pushed aside the curtain and scrambled into their tiny tenement. Reuben sat down on the sleeping pallet and tugged their threadbare blanket over his legs, shivering; his nose and lips were blue with cold. Juliette longed to light the fire, but she knew that Beatrice never allowed her to use up their precious bits of coal. Instead, she crawled under the blanket with him and wrapped her arms around him, and they snuggled down close together. She hadn't realized how very cold it had become outside.

Soon she heard the familiar weary tread of Beatrice's shoes on the hallway outside.

"If she asks, say we were home all day," she whispered to Reuben.

He nodded.

The curtain was brushed aside, and Beatrice stepped into the tenement. She was a short woman with broad hips and shoulders, their bones now jutting against her shapeless dress as it hung sadly from her thin body. Her hands were always red and sore, and her lumpish nose and watery grey eyes were reddened, too. Sometimes Juliette watched and tried to help when Beatrice washed their clothes, and her mother's face reminded her of the way she would twist and squeeze a wet dress to get the water out: she was wrung out, squeezed dry by life.

"Hello, children," said Beatrice. "Have you been good today?"

Juliette's throat closed, and she said nothing.

"Very good, Mama," said Reuben.

"That's good, Roo." Beatrice went over to the tiny, rickety table in the corner—one leg propped up by a wad of old newspaper—and set a paper bag down on it. She took a few small bits of coal from their rusty coal-scuttle and tipped them into the diminutive hearth, then lit them. Their faint glow was useless against the pervading cold as the mist sank like a grey curtain outside the window.

"I bought some vegetables for supper," she said.

"Thank you, Mama," said Juliette dutifully.

Beatrice sighed and stared out of the window for a few long moments. Then she squared her shoulders and turned back to the fire. Their only pot, which had a hole near the top and could never be more than half full, waited beside the fireplace. Beatrice hung it over the struggling coals and poured some water into it from the bucket in the corner. She grabbed the paper bag and hastily tipped the vegetables inside, but she was still slow enough that Juliette could count them: two beets, a carrot, and an onion.

Juliette rested a hand on her stomach and breathed out a silent prayer of thanks that she'd already filled her belly with bread. Reuben, too, wasn't staring at the pot with his usual hunger. His eyelids were drooping.

"What did you two get up to today?" Beatrice asked with forced cheerfulness. "Did you help Margie to clean the hallway again?"

"Not today, Mama," said Juliette. "We just stayed here."

"Margie's sick," said Reuben.

Beatrice's eyes widened, and she grabbed Reuben's arm. "Sick?" she cried. "What kind of sick? Is it a cough?"

"No, Mama," said Juliette. "It's the same thing that always happens to her, when she feels weak, and her face goes all blue and grey."

Beatrice relaxed visibly and let go of Reuben's arm. She went over to the bubbling pot and prodded at the vegetables with a fork that was missing one tine.

"Poor Margie," she said. "She's a lovely woman, but often ill. No wonder her husband won't let her work a stitch, and she always ends up alone here in the tenement."

"Why is she always alone?" Juliette asked. "She loves children. She should have some."

Beatrice sighed. "I don't think she can, dear."

"Why not?" Juliette asked.

"I don't know," said Beatrice. "Some women aren't as lucky as I am." She forced a thin smile.

Juliette returned it.

"That's why you must never, never go outside." Beatrice came over to the pallet and wrapped one arm around Juliette, then ruffled Reuben's hair as he slept. "There are people who can't have children, and some are good souls like Margie, but do you know what others do?"

"What?" Juliette asked.

"They steal children for themselves," said Beatrice. "They take them right off the streets and take them away from their mamas, and no one ever sees them again."

Juliette shuddered. She thought of the chill she'd felt standing in front of the alleyway that morning, and she swallowed hard.

"That's why you must always stay inside, all right, darling?" Beatrice squeezed her.

Juliette nodded. "All right."

A few minutes later, Beatrice drained the vegetables and put them on the table. "Suppertime." she said with forced cheerfulness, cutting them up.

Juliette glanced down at Reuben. Still cuddled beside her, he was fast asleep. She slipped out from under the blanket, carefully to avoid waking him, and joined Beatrice at the table.

"Bring your brother, Juli," said Beatrice sharply.

"I don't think he's hungry, Mama," said Juliette.

Beatrice's eyes widened. "Why not?" She gasped. "He's always hungry."

Juliette stared down into the pot. The whole vegetables, pale and wrinkled, looked better than nothing.

"Margie gave us some bread today," she lied. "He's just eaten."

Beatrice relaxed slightly. "That's kind of her," she said.

"So did I," Juliette added, "so I'm not very hungry, either."

Beatrice met her eyes. "Are you sure?"

"I'm sure," said Juliette.

She was still a *little* hungry, truth be told, and the half carrot and half beet that Beatrice gave her wasn't much. Still, she didn't regret it as she watched her mother bolting down the rest of the vegetables as fast as she could, as though she hadn't had a drop to eat for days.

Maybe that much was true. And that was why Juliette thought she couldn't stop going outside, ever.

It was the only way she could help her mother.

CHAPTER 3

Spring was a thing that seldom ever came to Whitechapel, even if the calendar made appointments for its arrival. It was as though sunshine itself couldn't be bothered to attempt to pierce the clouds of smog that hung over that part of the sprawling, brawling city, choked out by ships on the Thames and factories that belched smoke, steam and chemicals with every breath. Even in late May, the shadows always seemed to be on the brink of frost. Warmth seldom ever came to the muddy streets. Even the half-decent marketplace where Juliette and Reuben went begging was usually lit only by grubby, greyish light that seemed to flow sluggishly into the marketplace, as though it had already been half used up by the richer folk of London.

But today was a little different. Today, real sunshine had escaped the grip of the smoke and clouds, and it was pouring warm and bright onto Juliette's shoulders as she stood on their usual corner with Reuben's hand wrapped tightly in their own. His fingers sweated a little in hers, and she adjusted her grip slightly.

She glanced around the crowded marketplace for the umpteenth time that day, looking for Emory, but he was still in the same place he'd been since briefly greeting them that morning: on the corner opposite theirs. He carried a worn-out tray around his neck to display his pitiful wares; a few river pebbles washed smooth, a stone with a hole through the middle, a small pile of old rags he'd washed under the pump, and an empty glass bottle. Emory had hardly sold a thing all day, Juliette noted, and his eyes were worried as they darted around the crowd.

"Alms," Reuben called in his tiny piping voice. "Spare change for a poor child?" He parroted the line simply, just like Juliette had taught him.

An old lady, bent laboriously over a walking stick, stopped near them. "Where are your parents?" she wheezed.

"Mama's working," said Reuben. "Papa died."

"Oh, you poor mites." The old woman shook her bonneted head. "Tis a cruel, cruel world, even on a nice day like this." She fumbled in her purse with ancient fingers and withdrew an entire sixpence. "Here you are, love."

"Thank you." Juliette burst out.

Reuben mumbled, "Thank you."

The woman shuffled off, and Juliette grabbed the sixpence out of Reuben's hand. It was large and boldly shiny.

"Oh, Reuben, this is wonderful." she gasped.

"It's only one," said Reuben.

"Yes, but it's more than the ones you usually get," said Juliette.

Reuben frowned.

"Never mind that right now." Juliette grinned. "We can get something to eat right away." She glanced around the marketplace, her belly rumbling. She couldn't remember the last time they'd had meat, and her gaze darted from the old woman selling watery beef stew to the old man cooking fish over a fire.

"I'm hungry." Reuben tugged at her hand. "I want stew."

A cheerful young man strode up to the fishmonger. There was a brief exchange, and the fishmonger picked out a cooked fish and wrapped it in some old newspaper. Juliette's eyes locked onto the newspaper as the old man handed it over.

"We're getting fish," she said.

"But I want stew," Reuben whined.

"Well, we're getting fish this time," said Juliette firmly.

She tugged at her little brother's hand and led him up to the fishmonger. He was an old man with drooping cheeks and a hooked nose, and he regarded them sharply with dark eyes set far too close together.

"Go away," he snapped. "I won't tolerate beggars."

"We're not begging, sir," said Juliette politely, just like Margie had told her. "How much is a fish?"

The old man's eyes narrowed. "Eight pence."

Juliette breathed a sigh of relief. Reuben had been given tuppence before the sixpence, and she'd picked up a penny in the gutter on the way here. "We'll take one, please."

She pushed the money across the fishmonger's ramshackle table, and he glared at it suspiciously for a moment before he turned away and grabbed a sheaf of newspaper from the pile lying on the end of the table. Juliette's eyes focused hungrily on the words as they grew stained and crumpled while the fishmonger wrapped them around the piece of fish. But some of them survived, she saw. Some of them would still be readable.

"There," the fishmonger grunted, holding out the bundle wrapped in newspaper.

Juliette reached out to take it, then felt a sudden, jarring pang of cold run down her spine. She gasped and spun around, her heart suddenly pounding. Someone was staring at her, at both of them. She was certain of it. Her eyes skimmed through the marketplace, but she saw only haggling stallholders and sellers. Even the drunken old man in the grubby corner near the tannery was asleep, snoring, his head tilted back, flies buzzing around his open mouth.

"Your fish, child," the fishmonger growled.

"Thank you," Juliette gasped. She took the fish and tucked it under one arm, gripping Reuben's hand tightly. "Let's go."

They turned for home, and Juliette hesitated again and looked around the crowd. Still, she saw no one staring at her, but she'd been absolutely certain a few moments ago.

"Emory's hungry," said Reuben.

Juliette glanced at him. He was still on his corner, not watching her, but she saw that he was staring intently at the old woman with the stew. A bony man stopped and stared down at his tray; Emory gave him a bright smile and started to offer him the bottle for only ha'penny, but the man shook his head and walked away.

"Poor Emory," said Juliette. "Come on, Roo. Let's give him some fish and that penny that we didn't need."

Reuben nodded enthusiastically, and they crossed the marketplace carefully. Juliette glanced over her shoulder a few more times, but she didn't see anyone staring. Still, all the hairs on the back of her neck were standing up.

"Are you all right, Juli?" Emory asked as they reached him.

Juliette smiled. "Yes. Why?"

"You keep looking around like you think something's chasing you," said Emory.

"Oh, no... there's no one," said Juliette. She glanced back again, then shook herself. "Here. Have some fish."

Emory stared hungrily at the bundle in her hands. "Are you sure?" he asked.

"Yes, please. Have some," said Juliette. She opened one end of the parcel and tore off a generous chunk.

"Oh, thank you," Emory breathed. He set down the tray and took the fish in his grubby, blackened fingers. Dirt smeared onto the white flesh, but Emory didn't seem to care; he shoved it into his mouth and ate in huge, hungry gulps, then sucked every drop of oil from his fingers.

"I'm hungry," Reuben complained.

"Go on home," said Emory. "Eat before it gets cold." He smiled. "And thank you."

Juliette dug in her pocket for the penny she'd found and held it out. "Here... I don't need this today."

Emory stared at her, his smile gone. Juliette pressed the penny into his hand before he could protest.

"But—why?" he gasped. "Why would you give me this?"

Juliette smiled and thought of the three little rabbits, escaping their smelly marsh and gambolling away onto greener fields all together.

"For the stories," she said. "Come on, Roo."

She led her little brother away across the marketplace, and the further they walked, the more she felt as though a shadow was stalking after them. She thought of the chill that she'd felt the other day with her back to the alley, and she peered nervously into the alley as they passed it, just in case. But it was empty. And when she stopped at the street corner and looked back, she still saw no one staring, no one following her.

THE FISH WAS warm and satisfying in Juliette's stomach, but she couldn't shake the fear that had followed her all the way home. She tried to turn her attention to the scrap of newspaper clutched tightly in her hands. She'd torn it out of the ruined, oily paper that had been wrapped around the fish, but she was sure it was enough; Margie had taught her to tear neatly around the blocks of text, and she'd gotten a whole block out with hardly any stains.

Reuben tagged after her, his little feet shuffling on the floor. They stopped at Margie's door, and Juliette listened intently for a moment to make sure that her husband, Bert, wasn't home. Bert had a red nose and shouted when he saw the children sometimes. There was silence, so Juliette knocked, and when there was no response, she pushed the door open and peered inside. The tenement was empty.

"Where's she?" Reuben asked.

Juliette felt a pang of terror grip her belly, but then she heard the swish-swish of a broom on the staircase to their left. "I think I know," she said.

The children hurried to the landing, and sure enough, there was Margie, sweeping the steps. There were ugly dark stains here and there that seemed utterly impervious to the broom, but at least a small pile of dust was gathering as Margie worked her broom over a step near the middle.

"Margie," Reuben squealed, scampering down the steps to meet her.

"Oh, hello." Margie laughed and spread her arms. Reuben hugged her knees, and she returned the embrace. "How are you children today?"

"We're very well, Margie," said Juliette. "Look what I found."

She held up the paper, and Margie's bony face brightened. "Oh, a newspaper," she cried.

"Please help me," Juliette begged. "Please."

"Of course, darling. The only reason I don't teach you more often is because it's so hard to find anything to read." Margie leaned her broom against the wall and held out a hand. "Let me see."

Juliette proudly handed over her trophy, and Margie sat down on the step. There was a slight wheeze in her breathing, but her eyes were animated as they skimmed over the paper. Reuben and Juliette tucked themselves against her on either side, staring eagerly at the paper.

"All right, then," said Margie. "Can you name the letters, Juli?" She pointed to the first word in the headline.

Juliette frowned and sounded them out carefully. "F-I-R-E." She paused. "Fire."

"That's right." Margie grinned. "Keep going."

Slowly, Juliette went on. "D-E-S-T-R-O-Y-S. Des... tr... o... ees?"

"Destroys," Margie corrected gently. She sighed. "We really need a first reader, not newspaper articles. That word was too hard."

"It's not too hard." Juliette clenched her tiny fists. "I can do it." She took a deep breath. "Fire destroys... S-H-O-P. S-H means *sh*. Shop. Fire destroys shop."

"That's right." Margie's eyes danced, and she beamed. "Perfect."

Juliette giggled.

"You're so clever, Juli," Reuben breathed.

"It's because Margie taught me." Juliette gazed up into Margie's eyes. "She's the clever one."

"Teach me too," said Reuben eagerly.

Margie laughed. "You're a little small for that, Roo, but as soon as you're old enough, I'm sure Juliette will show you."

Juliette frowned. "You can show him too, Margie, when he's old enough."

Margie hesitated for a moment, then ruffled Reuben's hair, her smile thin. "Yes, I'm sure I can," she said faintly. She cleared her throat. "Did you two buy this in the marketplace?"

"It came with fish," said Reuben.

"I hope you're being very careful out there," said Margie.

Juliette shivered; her mind made up. "We're not going out again."

"What?" Reuben cried. "Why?"

"I just—I don't think it's safe," said Juliette. She thought of that creeping sensation, and her belly tied itself in knots. She thought of the frightening people that Beatrice kept telling them about, the ones who stole children and took them away from their mamas forever.

She'd vowed to herself then that they would never stop going outside, because she knew that it was the only way Beatrice ever got enough to eat. But what if someone took them? What would happen to Reuben, or to their mother?

"Are you all right, dear?" Margie asked.

Juliette swallowed. "I'm all right. Can we keep reading?"

"Of course, my poppet," said Margie. She put an arm around each of the children. "Let's try the first few words of the article, Juli."

Juliette forced her eyes to focus on the small black words on the page, even though her heart was fluttering wildly in her chest at the memory of that feeling of being followed.

"Po-lik," she read.

"Police," Margie murmured.

"Police are baff-led..." Juliette read.

She kept trying, but her thoughts were back in that marketplace, and she knew that she had no choice. It was better to be hungry than to be taken away from their mama.

⚜

REUBEN'S CRYING WOULDN'T STOP.

Juliette lay curled up on the sleeping pallet, her head on the cold, hard wood. She had the blanket wadded up over her ears, but she could still hear the thin drumming of the rain against the walls, the *plop* of rainwater tumbling into the bucket that they put beneath the leak, and the steady wail of Reuben's weeping.

The little boy staggered around the tenement, his pale face streaked with dirt and tears. His mouth was wide open, and the thin, keening cry emanated from him with every breath, the slow and constant weeping of a child who knew it would be hours before he had any reason to stop. His little voice was hoarse from crying now, but he still carried on.

"Roo, stop it, please," Juliette begged.

Reuben sat down sharply in the middle of the floor and pressed his dirty hands over his face. "Hungry," he wailed. "So hungry."

"I know," Juliette snapped. "I'm hungry, too." Her stomach felt as though it had shrivelled up and might blow away at any second. She tried to remember the last time they'd eaten more than a few scraps of fish or two boiled eggs each. Had it been a week? It could have been. The last time she'd had a full stomach was when she'd bought the fish at the marketplace, the week before last.

She rolled onto her side and wrapped her arms around her aching belly, trying to ignore Reuben's continued sobbing. Juliette pinched her eyes tightly shut. Reuben's keening cries felt as though they were piercing down into her soul, but the ache in the pit of her belly was much worse.

Somewhere in the building, someone coughed. Juliette's aching head spun, and she found herself drifting into a dream of the marketplace, all of its delicious smells, the food that was everywhere. She went up to a vendor who was selling fruits: beautiful, ruby-red apples, so brilliant and lovely that they could have been jewels. She took one and bit into it, and its sweet juice flooded her mouth and poured over her chin.

A sudden chill ran down Juliette's spine. She knew, again, that she was being watched. When she whipped around, the marketplace was gone, replaced by a massive shadow that towered over her. Its eyes glowed red, and it swooped toward her face. Reuben screamed—

Juliette sat up, gasping. She could still taste that apple, but the dampness on her chin was from her own saliva, not apple juice. Reuben screamed again, his hands pressed to his belly, and rocked back and forth.

"What is it?" Juliette demanded angrily. Her limbs felt weak and trembly.

"Sore," Reuben whimpered. "So sore."

They were hunger pangs, Juliette knew. She tasted that phantom apple again and wanted to scream herself. When she pressed her hands to her belly, she could feel it grumbling.

But what about that red-eyed shadow? What about the thing Juliette had felt in that marketplace?

She leaned against the wall, sweating and shaky, and Reuben screamed once more. Margie had given them a few slices of bread yesterday, but even with Margie's help, there just wasn't enough to go around.

The red-eyed shadow wasn't real, Juliette realized. Maybe the feeling of being watched wasn't either.

But Reuben's screams were far too real.

"All right." Juliette got to her feet, then clutched at the wall as a wave of dizziness assailed her. "All right," she said again. "Come on, Roo. We're going out to find food."

Reuben's screams stopped instantly. He stared up at her, round-eyed. "We are?"

"Yes." Juliette reached out a hand. "Come on."

The little boy snatched at her fingers, and they shuffled out of the room and into the great, hungry city.

CHAPTER 4

JULIETTE'S SKIN crawled as they hurried toward the tenement building. The loaf of bread she had clutched in her hands was still warm, and she and Reuben tore chunks out of it as they walked, gulping them down while they pushed through the crowd. But now, standing on the pavement opposite the building, Juliette suddenly stopped chewing.

"Juli, give me," Reuben complained, reaching up toward the loaf of bread.

"Shhh," Juliette hissed. She whipped around, her heart hammering, but there was no one there. Only the old man with the rheumy eyes who always leaned against the wall. He was lying in a puddle of last night's rainwater, but he didn't seem to care. He never seemed to care about anything.

He wasn't the red-eyed shadow, Juliette thought, but the shadow was real. She'd felt it watching her.

"Come on, Roo," she hissed.

She tugged sharply at her brother's hand and ignored his yelps as she dashed across the street. A man on a bicycle nearly ran her over, but she ducked him, ignoring his yells, and shoved open the door of the tenement building. They stumbled inside and Juliette slammed the door behind them and stood, trembling, peering through the keyhole.

She saw no one coming across the street toward them.

"Give me," Reuben wailed, reaching for the bread.

Juliette's racing heart slowed. She allowed him to pull off a chunk of the bread, then gripped his hand and led him up the stairs. They paused at Margie's door, and Juliette knocked.

Margie opened it at once. Her hands were wet and soapy to the elbows, and she wasn't wearing her coat; she shivered. "Ah, children, there you are." She smiled. "I see you've bought some bread."

"Yes," said Juliette. "Do you want some?"

A cough somewhere on their floor echoed down the hallway. It had a strange sound to it, like barking, and Margie stiffened. She listened for a few long moments, then turned back to Juliette, her smile returning.

"No thank you, dear." She ruffled Reuben's hair. "Enjoy it."

"I'll help you with your washing tomorrow," Juliette promised.

"You're such a poppet." Margie kissed her forehead. "Off you go."

Juliette and Reuben scampered into their tenement, sat down on the sleeping pallet and tore great pieces off the loaf of bread, then stuffed them into their mouths. In just a few minutes, the loaf was gone, and Juliette's stomach was sore and tight. Still, this was a far better soreness than the aching emptiness of just a while ago.

They curled up on the pallet against each other, and Reuben's breathing was quiet and even. Juliette listened to the barking cough. It seemed to be coming from a different direction now, and it never seemed to stop.

"Juli?" Reuben whispered.

Juliette jumped. She'd thought he was asleep. "What is it, Roo?"

Her brother looked up at her. Some colour had returned to his cheeks. "Thank you."

Juliette held him closer and pressed her face into his dirty hair. "I'm sorry," she whispered. "I'm sorry I kept us inside."

But she remembered the creeping feeling, the certainty that the red-eyed shadow was behind her and knew that she would have to be vigilant if she wanted to go on feeding her brother.

FOOTSTEPS JOLTED Juliette awake a few hours later. They were fast and heavy—someone running in the hallway.

Instantly, Juliette sat up and grabbed Reuben by the back of his coat. It was seldom, in this place of the weary and hopeless, that anyone ever ran, but when they did, it was never good news. The last time someone had come running down the hallway, it had been a young man with no teeth and only a few crazy tufts of hair, swinging a piece of broken glass and shrieking about spiders no one else could see. He'd cut old Mr. Kennedy's arm grievously before he launched himself from a window and fell to his death on the street below.

"Juli?" Reuben whimpered.

"Stay behind me," Juliette hissed.

The curtain to the tenement swung aside, and Juliette braced herself. But there was no opium-addled madman here. It was only Beatrice, her eyes very wide, her breaths coming in great gasps. Sweat soaked into her grimy bonnet, and she was shaking.

"Mama." Juliette released Reuben. "Are you all right?"

"Oh, my children, my children," Beatrice cried. She flung herself down on the pallet beside them and threw her arms around them both. Juliette found herself being crushed into her mother's bony chest. "My children," Beatrice wailed.

"Mama?" Juliette whimpered. "What's the matter?"

"It's here," said Beatrice. "Don't you hear it? It's here."

Juliette's thoughts flew to the red-eyed shadow. They all three fell totally silent, listening. Juliette wondered how it would sound: would there be the scrape of claws on the floor? The swish of a dreadful cloak? Total silence as it stalked them?

Instead, there was no sound except for the howl of the wind in the holes that peppered the walls, and that strange cough. It was a harsh, hacking sound, followed by a high-pitched, whistling struggle to suck in another breath.

Juliette realized that there was more than one person coughing in this building. There were many, above and below, all around.

"It's here," Beatrice whispered.

"What is it, Mama?" Juliette quavered.

Beatrice sat back. Her pale eyes were very large, and her hands were shaking as she clutched the children.

"Whooping cough," she whispered. "The thing that killed your father."

Juliette's heart froze within her. She knew Reuben didn't remember Papa, but she did, distantly. She remembered that his beard tickled her cheek when he kissed her and that he had a big, jolly laugh. She also remembered there was a time before Papa was gone when they lived in a cosy cottage, and she had her own bed and dolls to play with.

She clutched at Beatrice's hands. Whooping cough had taken all of that from her, and now she heard it surrounding them.

"What is it?" Reuben asked.

"It's an illness, pet." Beatrice shuddered. "It's a dreadful, dreadful illness that takes everything from you and leaves you alone and scared." She lowered her voice to a hoarse whisper. "And it spreads like wildfire. It's in the air of this place now."

Reuben held his breath. Juliette wanted to do the same thing.

"Are we going to die, Mama?" Juliette whispered.

Beatrice's eyes flashed. "No, darling, you are not," she said firmly. "Because you are going to stay right here in this room, do you understand? You are not to go out into the hallway or even pull the curtain aside for anyone. If you do, the whooping cough will get you."

Reuben nodded fiercely, his eyes very wide.

"What about Margie?" Juliette asked.

Beatrice's face fell. "Margie and Bert will have to make do without you. You will go nowhere. Nowhere."

"Yes, Mama," Juliette whispered, thinking of the scrap of newspaper she'd picked up on a street corner. She'd so looked forward to reading it with Margie.

"I'm scared," said Reuben.

"You'll be safe in here, my love." Beatrice stroked his hair. "You'll be safe."

"But what about you, Mama?" Juliette asked.

Beatrice squared her shoulders. "I must go to work, pet, or we'll starve. But I shall also be looking for a new place to stay. Somewhere far away from here." She shivered. "Far from *this*."

There was another long silence, and one person coughed distantly. Juliette thought the whooping sound they made between coughs sounded like someone being suffocated.

It sounded like death.

CHAPTER 5

THERE WAS nothing to do now except to sit at the window.

Juliette leaned her forehead against the glass and stared down at the street outside. Reuben had finally stopped crying for food; he was asleep on the pallet now, curled on his side, his knees drawn up to his chest, clean trails washed on his grubby cheeks by the tears. In a few hours he would wake again and sob for food. Juliette hoped Beatrice would be back by then. Even the meagre scraps she brought home, the chewy sausages and the stale bread, were far better than nothing.

Around her, whooping cough echoed.

Juliette closed her eyes and thought of Margie. When she reached into the pocket of her ragged dress, she could still feel the piece of newspaper she'd folded up and tucked away there. The edges were all soft and crinkled from her constant fingering; soon she wouldn't be able to make out the letters. She'd practiced sounding them out, even stringing together some of the words, but it just wasn't the same. Many of them were far too hard for her.

She thought of Margie, pale and blue. She didn't know anything about whooping cough, but she wondered, if you were already sick, what another sickness would do to you. Juliette couldn't help but wonder if it made you even sicker.

She opened her eyes again and saw that the terrible wagon had come up to the front door of the building again, the black one drawn by the ribby dark horses, the one with the black cover. The front door opened, and two men went inside. They came out a little bit later, carrying a bony, ragged figure. The man's head lolled back uselessly. The other two men threw him into the back of the wagon like he was a sack of dung.

Juliette held her breath as the men returned to the building. They each came out carrying tiny bundles, no bigger than Reuben, which they laid inside the wagon without reverence. Then they climbed onto the driver's seat and drove away.

Juliette let out a breath. The men who took away the dead people had not taken away any women today. That had to mean that Margie was still alive.

Another desperate, struggling cough echoed through the building. It was on their own floor, Juliette was certain. Perhaps it was Margie. Perhaps, tomorrow, the men would take her away, too, and throw her into the back of that wagon never knowing that she was the one who swept the stairwells and knocked the cobwebs from the windows and taught skinny little girls how to read.

Juliette let out a soft moan at the very thought. She looked up and down the street, looking for Beatrice, even though she knew it was still hours before her mother would come home. Beatrice had been staying away longer and longer recently, searching for a new home that they could move to. Often it was very dark before Beatrice finally came home. Still, Juliette's eyes roved across the street, searching and searching, seeing no one familiar in the crush of people scurrying along the muddy street. She noticed that all of them gave their own tenement building a wide berth. They knew death lurked there.

Then, her eyes caught on something, a splash of colour, a brightness. She sat up straighter and squinted. What was it? It had made her soul light up just briefly, as though a sunbeam had struck her despite the grey sky.

She saw it again—saw *him* again.

It was Emory.

He stood on the pavement opposite the tenement building, staring up at the windows, his eyes scanning the facade as though he was looking for something. There was no smile on his face now, but Juliette knew him instantly, the way she knew the moon in the sky. She pressed a hand against the glass, her heart pounding. Emory looked well: bony as ever, of course, but there was colour in his cheeks, and his eyes looked bright even at a distance. His tray, as usual, was around his neck, but he barely seemed interested in the passing crowds. He was looking at the building.

He was, Juliette realized, looking for her.

"Oh, Emory," she whispered.

Stories below, he didn't hear her. He stepped forward and crossed the street, weaving between the pedestrians, and stepped out into the clear space in front of the building. Juliette's heart froze.

"Stop!" She gasped.

A stranger caught at Emory's arm, an old woman. She was shaking her head violently, and she pointed up at the building, talking fast. Emory asked her something, and she shook her head again, then plucked at his sleeve. Reluctantly, Emory turned and walked away, glancing back at the tenement every few moments.

Juliette felt a wave of relief wash over her. Then she pressed her head against the window, closed her eyes, and wept.

IT WAS VERY LATE, and almost utterly dark in the tenement. The only light came from the smouldering coals in the tenement next door, their faint glow oozing beneath the flimsy wooden partition that celebrated the rooms. Often, the man and woman next door argued, and Reuben and Juliette would listen to their shouting. But tonight, there was no sound. No coughing. Only soft sobs sometimes.

Juliette stared at the strips of light above and below that partition until her eyes hurt. It was better than looking anywhere else; the room was in total darkness, and if she allowed herself to look into it, she would begin to feel as though she had never existed. Wind shrieked around the building and stuck its cold, bony fingers through the gaps in the wall, tickling the back of Juliette's neck.

She tried to stop her teeth from chattering and wrapped their only blanket a little more firmly around herself and Reuben. He snuggled closer against her chest, crying softly. She wondered if she had ever been as hungry as she was right now. Reuben had been crying incessantly since he woke hours ago.

The tread of footsteps sounded on the hallway, and Juliette slowly raised her head. The curtain was brushed aside, and light from the hallway flooded the room. The silhouette in the doorway was Beatrice's.

"Mama." Juliette jumped to her feet.

Reuben scrambled toward her on his hands and knees and tugged at the hem of her dress. "Mama, you brought food?" he asked.

There was a long silence, and Juliette didn't understand. Why didn't Mama rush inside and hold them?

Finally, Beatrice spoke. "Children... I'm sorry." She shuffled into the room and fumbled for a match to light a stub of candle; it was only to be used for cooking, never at other times, and Beatrice always had the matches in her pocket.

Juliette gasped at the sight of her mother's face. It was utterly pale, the cheeks deathly sunken, and her eyes were watery and rimmed with red.

"Mama, are you all right?" she asked.

"Fire," Beatrice croaked, as though reminding herself. She shuffled to the fireplace, fell to her knees, and produced a few sticks of dampish wood from her canvas bag. She started to arrange them in the fireplace.

"Food?" Reuben whimpered.

"Bread... in the bag," Beatrice whispered.

Reuben and Juliette fell upon the bag. They ripped it open and found four bread rolls, once white and soft, now so stale that they felt like rocks in Juliette's hand. But they were still food; when she raised one to her nose, it still held traces of the hearty bread smell. Reuben immediately began crunching into his.

"Here, Mama," said Juliette, holding one out to Beatrice.

Beatrice turned her face away. "No... no."

Juliette's heart stuttered in her chest. She held the roll a little closer to her mother. "Mama, it's food."

"I'm not hungry," Beatrice whispered.

Juliette stared at her. "What?"

Beatrice ignored her. She stumbled over to the sleeping pallet and sank down upon it, then pulled the blanket over her shoulder.

Reuben didn't seem to notice. He was tearing into his bread roll, but Juliette couldn't take her eyes off Beatrice. There was something strange about the way she breathed, slowly and carefully, as though she was trying to prevent something.

"Mama?" Juliette whispered.

Beatrice didn't respond. The faint bread smell was still rising from the roll in Juliette's hand, and she raised it to her lips, unable to resist it anymore. She bit into it, food blessedly filling her mouth even if it was hard and dry.

She was chewing her second bite when Beatrice lifted her head and sucked in a long, rattling breath.

Then she coughed. A low, hacking sound.

Accompanied by a high-pitched whoop as she inhaled.

CHAPTER 6

JULIETTE'S small hands shook on the pail of cold water as she crouched down beside Beatrice. The pail was nearly empty, even though she had been so, so careful to keep wringing out the rag into it. She didn't know what would happen when the water ran out. It was already murky and brownish, and tasted bitter when she and Reuben sipped from the pail, half a cup at a time, trying desperately to make it last.

Beatrice wouldn't let them leave the tenement, not even to pump water.

Juliette tried not to think about that. She dipped her grubby rag in the water and wrung it out, careful to make sure that every drop fell back into the pail. Then she pressed the cool, damp rag against Beatrice's forehead.

Beatrice's eyes fluttered open. They were fevered pits in her head, her skin flushed and dotted with sweat.

"No," she moaned.

"It's all right, Mama," said Juliette gently. "It's helping." She had no idea if it was helping or not; she just knew that Beatrice had done this to Reuben when he'd had a cold as a little baby. It was the only thing she could think to do.

Beatrice sucked in a breath and another fit of coughing gripped her bony frame, making it twitch and jerk heartlessly, that dreadful whoop punctuating each cough. The fits were so violent that they seemed at risk of ripping the sinews from her protruding bones.

Juliette glanced over at the mat near the stove. Reuben was curled up on it, asleep after a full night of crying. It had been two days since either of them had last eaten, and Juliette wanted to cry too. Instead, she dipped the rag back in the water and wrung it out again.

Beatrice opened her eyes once more when Juliette pressed the rag to her forehead.

"Mama, are you awake?" Juliette whispered.

Beatrice hardly seemed to know herself anymore. For the past day, she had been drifting somewhere between asleep and awake, in a fevered, painful dreamland. The only consistent thing was the coughing.

"Yes," she whispered.

"I heard the people next door say that they were going to buy medicine," said Juliette. "There must be medicine that can help you. I should go and get some."

"No," Beatrice rasped.

"Please, Mama." Juliette's eyes swam with tears. "I'm so worried. You're not getting better. What if you never get better?"

The thought was intolerable.

"No," snapped Beatrice.

"Isn't there any money in your bag?" Juliette whispered. "We need food, too. You need some soup... maybe then—"

"There's nothing," Beatrice snapped, her words hoarse and hollow. "There's nothing left. I'm sorry."

Juliette stared at her mother. She knew that, in just a few days, the sallow-faced man would come for the money that they paid to have somewhere to live. And then what?

"Mama..." she began.

"Nothing. I'm sorry," Beatrice whispered.

She rolled over then, turning her back on Juliette, and fell asleep. Juliette dropped the rag back into the bucket and curled up beside her mother. Her body shook, and she felt so weak, so empty. When she pressed her hands over her face, she felt how cold they were.

She wanted to cry, but she couldn't form any tears. Her heart thumped helplessly in her chest. All around her, whooping cough echoed from wall to wall, filling the tenement building utterly.

She couldn't go outside and beg. The red-eyed shadow was the least of their worries now.

"I'M GOING," Reuben announced.

Juliette raised her aching head from their pillow on her arms. She was kneeling beside Beatrice on the sleeping pallet, her head and arms resting on her mother's body, feeling the slow, rattling rhythm of her breathing. Her head felt too heavy to hold up.

"What?" she mumbled.

Reuben was standing at the curtain of the tenement, trembling from head to toe. He clenched his small fists. "I'm going."

"Where?" Juliette whispered.

"To beg. They'll give us money. I'm hungry," Reuben whispered.

Juliette stared at him, struggling to muster the energy for a response. She wondered if anyone would even give them money now if they went outside. Reuben had always been so beautiful, but now his cheeks were pinched and grey, his eyes unnaturally large in his head. His hair was so dirty that it was caked against his head. He didn't look beautiful anymore; he looked sick and sad and scared and starving.

"No," she managed. "You can't go outside. You'll get sick."

"I'm hungry," Reuben insisted.

"Roo, don't touch that curtain," Juliette warned.

Beatrice moaned on the sleeping pallet, but her eyes didn't open. Juliette stroked her mother's sticky hair. Beatrice coughed twice, weakly, then stopped moving except for her struggling breaths.

"I'm hungry," said Reuben, and reached for the curtain.

"Stop that," Juliette screamed at him. "Stop right now."

Her shriek tore through the tenement and startled her almost as much as it startled him. He flung himself backward with a yelp. She'd never screamed at him like this before, and he immediately thrust his little fists into his eyes and began to cry.

Juliette staggered to her feet. "Don't cry, Roo." She reached toward him, but he retreated and tucked himself into the corner beside Beatrice, sobbing brokenheartedly.

Juliette closed her eyes. She stood swaying in the middle of the floor, trying to think. How could she find medicine for Beatrice? What was she going to do to feed her brother?

Maybe he could stay inside, and she would go out and beg on her own. She never had as much luck as he did, but Beatrice would always hate her if she allowed Reuben to go outside. If Reuben fell ill. If Reuben—

Juliette wouldn't allow herself to think of her brother dying. She opened her eyes and reeled over to the window instead. Pressing her forehead against the cold glass made her feel slightly more awake, and she blinked down at the usual crowd slogging through the muddy street. Maybe one of them would have some money or medicine they would give her. Maybe she wouldn't have to go any further than the front door.

Then she saw him. Emory.

He was standing on the pavement as usual, and again his face was turned up toward Juliette's building. But he looked very, very different from the rosy-cheeked boy she'd seen just a couple of weeks ago. In fact, Juliette only recognized him because of the tray around his neck. The brightness that usually surrounded him seemed to have vanished; instead, he stood shivering, his face drawn and ashen, hardly sparing a glance for the people who passed him by, let alone the smiles and kind words that usually drew them in. There was only a single piece of broken glass on the tray in front of him. No one spared him a second glance.

Juliette pressed her hand against the glass. "Emory," she whispered.

Of course, he didn't hear her. But it almost seemed like a response when he raised his hand to his face and began to cough. Juliette didn't need to be able to hear the cough to know it. It was just as violent as Beatrice's, harsh and ripping, as though it would tear his slender little body apart.

Juliette sank down to her knees, then to her side on the cold floor. She drew her knees up to her chest and hugged them, and she wept with all her heart.

⚕

BEATRICE'S BODY SPASMED. Her head was flung back against the sleeping pallet with an audible thump, and her legs stretched out, straining, the bones of her feet showing white against her skin. She opened her mouth, but there was no sound.

"Mama!" Juliette cried. "Mama, wake up."

She shook her mother, but Beatrice's face was turning blue. Her eyes were blank and glassy, and her mouth opened even wider, but still there was no sound.

Finally, a thin, wailing breath entered Beatrice's lungs. She fell back, exhausted, and sucked in another breath, then another. Then she was coughing again, but the sound was weak now, desperate, as though her aching body could no longer bring itself to breathe.

Reuben sat in a corner. Juliette glanced at him, expecting that he would cry hysterically, but instead the little boy was simply motionless. He sat with his knees drawn up and his chin resting on them, arms draped limply beside him. His eyes were almost as glassy as Beatrice's.

"Roo?" Juliette left her mother and approached the boy, then reached out to touch his arm. "Roo, are you all right?"

Reuben rolled his eyes to stare at her, but he didn't speak. His lips were chapped and bleeding, but the pail was empty now, and he didn't say a word.

Juliette sank to the floor on her knees, trembling. She was so weak, and she knew that her brother must be feeling the same. Beatrice's terrible, ragged breathing was barely audible above the dread coughing that still filled the building. The coughing was less now, Juliette noted dully. So many people had stopped.

She wondered if they were better or dead. She wondered if they would all be dead soon.

Reuben closed his eyes and let out a tiny sound. It was half sob, half sigh, tiny and pitiful, and it ripped something open inside Juliette's heart.

"Margie," she whispered.

Reuben said nothing, but he stared at her.

"Margie." Juliette struggled to her feet. "Margie will help."

Reuben went to rise, but Juliette pushed him down again. "No. You're not coming."

"Juli—" Reuben croaked.

"Stay here, Roo," Juliette ordered.

She knew that he stayed not because he was obedient but because he was nearly too weak to walk. She knew this because *she* was nearly too weak to walk, and her knees wobbled as she staggered over to the curtain that formed their door. Her feet felt numb and distant as she pushed the curtain aside and stepped into the hallway.

She had never seen the hallway like this before. Grubby and stained. The floor covered in a layer of dirt. Cobwebs in all the corners.

Juliette sank to her knees again. She wanted to cry, but only a long wheeze of dismay would escape her. Was Margie dead, too? She nearly lay down right where she was, closed her eyes and let fate have its way with her, but she couldn't. Reuben needed her. The look in his eyes compelled her at least to try.

She drove herself to her feet and staggered forward, her feet sounding as hollow on the hallway as her stomach felt. When she reached Margie's door, it was closed, and she somehow gathered the strength to knock.

There was no response.

Juliette bit back a sob that she didn't have the strength for. She raised her hand and knocked again. "Margie," she croaked. "Margie... it's me."

There was a rustling behind the door. "Juliette?" Margie gasped. "Oh, poppet, how lovely to hear your voice." Footsteps hastened across the floor toward her.

Tears sprang to Juliette's eyes. She pressed her hands against the door. "Oh, Margie, please help me," she sobbed out. "Mama's sick, and I think she's going to die."

"My poor, poor poppet." The doorknob turned.

"Margaret!" a voice barked from inside the tenement. It was a low, hoarse, harsh voice, and the doorknob immediately stopped turning.

"Yes, Bert, darling?" Margie quavered. Her voice sounded altogether different to the way it usually did; it was as though all the sunshine had gone out of it.

"What are you doing?" Bert snarled.

"Margie, please," Juliette sobbed.

"I'm just talking to one of the two dear little children I told you about," said Margie. "She's outside, and it sounds like she's in trouble."

"You'll not open that door, woman," Bert snapped. "How do you expect to bear me a child if you're forever catching diseases from those appalling little urchins?"

"But Bert—" Margie began.

"I'll have none of it," Bert growled.

The sound of his voice made Juliette cower. He sounded so mean and cruel. She couldn't imagine why someone like Margie would marry someone like him. Dully, she realized that it must be a Sunday morning if Bert was home; he worked every other day.

"All right, dear," Margie croaked. "I... I won't open the door."

There was an unhappy grunt from behind her and then sloshing, like someone sipping from a bottle.

"Margie, please," Juliette whispered.

"Juli, sweetheart, I need you to go back into your tenement, all right?" said Margie.

Juliette fell to her knees with a thump, sobbing. "Please. Please. We're starving. I think Mama's going to die."

"I'm sorry, poppet." Margie's voice broke. "But there's nothing I can do for you. Please... go back inside the tenement and shut the curtain, all right? Just go back inside now."

"Margie," Juliette sobbed.

"Get rid of that urchin or I'll get rid of her!" Bert roared.

Juliette scrambled to her feet with a sob.

"I'm sorry, dear," Margie whispered.

Heavy footsteps echoed on the floor, and Margie gasped. Terrified, Juliette sprang to her feet and scrambled back to her own room with a strength she hadn't thought she had. She pulled the curtain shut behind her and stood inside, heart racing, but Bert didn't give chase.

When she looked around the room, she was almost surprised to see that Beatrice was still breathing. Reuben was still sitting in the corner. His face brightened when she saw Juliette, then travelled to her empty hands, and resumed its deathly dullness.

Nausea bucked in Juliette's empty stomach, but there was nothing to retch up. Her world swam, and she slumped slowly to the floor.

She woke hours later, her body stiff and aching, her cheek sore from being pressed against the cold floor. But when she sat up and pulled aside the curtain, there was half a loaf of bread wrapped in brown paper and a small canteen of water waiting outside.

CHAPTER 7

JULIETTE SLEPT THAT NIGHT, really slept, for the first time in
days.

The bread was more than enough given that only Juliette and
Reuben ate. Beatrice, shivering and coughing on the pallet,
could not wake enough to realize that there was food in front
of her. Juliette and Reuben tore the half-loaf into two pieces
and ate until they could eat no more. They finished every
scrap, but colour finally returned to Reuben's cheeks, and he
fell asleep almost at once, curled on the floor in the corner.

Juliette stayed awake a little longer. Strength returned to her
limbs once she'd eaten, and she found it in her to try to feed
Beatrice tiny sips of water from the canteen. Her lips were so
chapped and parched, and her mouth was open as she sucked
in tiny, desperate, rattling breaths between her coughs. Juli-

ette dripped water gently onto her tongue, and Beatrice smacked her lips and swallowed convulsively, as though her body knew its great need for water. She kept drinking until the canteen was half empty, and then Juliette tried to give her a bigger sip, feeling that the constant tiny swallows were sapping Beatrice's strength. She slopped water into her mouth, and Beatrice sucked in a breath that sounded like someone drowning. Her eyes popped wide open, glassy and unseeing, and she rolled onto her side, retching and choking.

Reuben sat up with a cry. Juliette slapped her mother's back, crying, "Mama! Mama!"

It seemed like an eternity before the choking finally stopped. Beatrice rolled onto her other side, her face putty-grey, lips ringed with blue. She lay still then, shivering, and her breathing sounded worse than ever.

Juliette didn't know if she'd done something to make her mother even sicker, but she was so tired, and it was so good to have a full belly that she struggled to care. She stoppered the canteen and curled up on the pallet behind Beatrice's back. The ravaging fever made her so warm that, even without the blanket, Juliette fell asleep almost instantly.

She slept the sleep of one with a full belly that night, deep and black and restful. Even the coughing that echoed through the building couldn't wake her. Instead, it was Reuben, shaking her shoulders and screaming her name, that jerked her from her sleep.

Juliette sat up, disoriented, her limbs stiff and her head aching. She couldn't tell what time it was, but it was very dark. There was a sliver of light from the streetlamp outside falling through the grubby window, and by its light she saw that Reuben's eyes were huge and round.

"Juli, Juli," he sobbed out.

"What?" Juliette gasped.

Reuben's eyes welled up with tears. "It's Mama," he said.

Juliette flew to her feet and lit the candle with the box of matches she'd stolen from Beatrice's pocket days ago. What she saw by the candlelight made her heart freeze within her.

For days, Beatrice's body had been racked by spasms, coughs, and twitches. Now, she lay utterly, absolutely still, her face waxy. Her eyes were half open, staring at nothing. She did not blink.

"Mama!" Juliette screamed. She set down the candle on the floor and flung herself onto her knees on the pallet. "Mama!"

"I tried. She won't—" Reuben sobbed. "She won't wake up."

Juliette's heart galloped in her chest. She clutched at Beatrice's hand, half expecting it to be stiff and lifeless. Instead, there was still some warmth left in it. Juliette flung herself down with her ear on her mother's chest and heard it: the faint, distant fluttering of a failing heart.

"Is she dead?" Reuben cried.

"No. No, she's not," said Juliette. "But—but she's dying."

Reuben's face contorted with terror. "Noooooo," he wailed. "Mama, nooooooo."

He threw himself over his mother's body and clutched at her dress with tiny hands, screaming and crying.

They needed help. Juliette knew it. Margie had brought them bread, but she knew that Bert wouldn't let her come here and help Beatrice. It didn't matter now; it couldn't matter now. Juliette needed to find help no matter who was willing to give it.

She stumbled into the hallway. "Help," she screamed. "Help. Help me."

Nothing stirred, and there was no sound except for the echo of her cry and for the dread coughing that still rattled around the building. Juliette stumbled up to the nearest actual door and hammered on it with all of her might. "Help," she screamed. "Help!"

The door swung open, and an old man with a hairy wart on his nose glared down at her. "Shut up, child," he snarled.

"My mama," Juliette wept. "Please. She won't wake up. Please help her."

"There's no help for her," the man snapped. "There's no help for anyone. She's going to die." He slammed the door.

The words felt like icicles piercing Juliette's heart. *She's going to die.* It couldn't be true. It couldn't. Who would feed them if she died? Who would give the man his rent money? Who would sing Reuben to sleep and wrap her arms around Juliette and smile even when her eyes looked distant and watery, just to see the children laugh?

"Help!" Juliette sobbed. She stumbled to the next door. "Please, help."

This time, the door didn't open, no matter how much Juliette knocked. She realized that there was a terrible, decaying smell coming from within, and her skin crawled. Fleeing, she rushed to the tenement across the hall; this one only had a curtain like hers, so she knocked on the wall beside it instead.

"What's this racket?" a woman snapped, pulling the curtain aside.

"Please, my mama's sick and she won't wake up," Juliette begged. "Help her. Please help her."

"She's dead already," said the woman. "Go back inside. You're spreading the disease. Do you want to kill us all just like your mother?"

She yanked the curtain closed again. Juliette stumbled back and turned, looking for another door to knock on. A silhouette behind her caught her eye, and she whipped around, the red-eyed shadow looming large in her mind. Instead, it was a bent little old woman who stood in the doorway behind her.

The hand that rested on the doorknob was little more than bones. She had tufts of white hair standing out explosively on her head. She wore a tattered collection of rags that might have been a dress once, and her face was so puckered, so wrinkled, so brutally blasted by life that it hardly seemed like a face at all.

Her eyes, however, ran Juliette through. They were massive and dark in the candlelight, and their focus was so intense that Juliette froze like a rabbit faced with a fox.

"Run home, girl," the woman whispered. Her voice sounded like the cold wind blowing through the holes in the walls. "Run home. Give up. Your mother will die soon."

Her gaze was so chilling that Juliette's courage failed her. She turned and dashed back to their tenement, her small feet pounding painfully on the floor. When she stumbled inside and pulled the curtain shut behind her, the look in Reuben's eyes stopped her in her tracks.

The little boy lay with his head on Beatrice's chest. She wasn't moving, and Reuben's face was a twisted, transfixed caricature of terror.

"I don't hear it," he whimpered. "I don't hear it."

Juliette sprinted to the pallet. She shoved Reuben aside and slammed her ear down on Beatrice's chest.

But she didn't hear it either.

The faint, fluttering efforts of Beatrice's heart had stopped.

THE MEN with the wagon came to take Beatrice away the next morning, very early.

Juliette and Reuben huddled in the corner, watching. Someone must have told the men that Beatrice was dead, because their heavy footsteps clumped unerringly up to the tenement. They came inside and glanced at the children, but their eyes slid over them as though they were only pieces of furniture.

The bigger one bent down and grabbed Beatrice's arms. They moved strangely, stiff as a doll's.

"No," Reuben spluttered.

Juliette flung her arms around him and wrestled him into her lap.

"Leave her alone," Reuben screamed.

The shorter of the two men turned his head to stare at Reuben. His eyes were rimmed with red, and there was cruelty in them.

"Roo, hush," Juliette hissed.

The other man stepped back, dragging Beatrice with him. Her head thudded on the floor as he dragged her off the pallet.

"Mama," Reuben cried.

The man glared harder. Juliette clapped a hand over Reuben's mouth and forced him down into her lap. He squirmed and whimpered but could do nothing as the men dragged Beatrice away. Juliette released him when the curtain swung shut, but he didn't try to run after his mother's body. Instead, his little head fell onto Juliette's shoulder, and he clung to her, sobbing, the way he always used to cling to Beatrice.

Juliette squeezed her eyes tightly shut and hung onto him, too, but it was her mother that she longed to hold in her arms.

***

MARGIE HAD LEFT bread outside the door in the night again. The men who fetched Beatrice had knocked it aside, but mercifully, they hadn't noticed it. Juliette wiped the dirt from the crust and gave it all to Reuben; he ate until he fell asleep on the pallet, his little body looking very small there all on its own, a chunk of crust still clutched in his small fist.

She stood by the window, unable to eat, shaking too hard to sleep. It was Monday morning, pale grey and bitterly cold.

Outside, smog hung so low and heavy that she couldn't tell if it was maybe rain. Condensation glittered on the grimy window, making it difficult to see outside into the blurry street. Juliette wiped some of the glass clean and stared out without seeing anything, searching for a familiar figure, bent with work, bonnet-wearing. She knew that her mother was never coming back again, but she still stared until her eyes hurt.

And the sallow-faced man stalked through her mind.

He would be here soon, just after dark, she was certain. He would demand the money that Beatrice gave him every Monday for rent. Juliette didn't even know how much it was, but she knew Beatrice always worried about being able to pay it.

There was no money in the tenement. Not a penny.

Juliette had seen people evicted from the building before. She'd seen some that screamed and begged and clutched at the doorframes until the sallow-faced man struck their fingers with his cane until they bled. She'd seen how they stumbled off, weeping. The other kind, the ones who took themselves away quietly, with their backs still straight and their heads held high, were more heart-breaking still.

Juliette didn't know what it would be like to be without a home, but the thought made her stomach tie itself in knots. Where would they go if it rained? Where would they sleep?

How would she keep her brother alive?

She glanced back at him where he lay on the pallet, and her hands clenched into skinny fists by her sides. She was all that Reuben had left now, and she knew, deep into the marrow of her bones, that whether he lived or died all depended on her.

"I won't let anything happen to you," she whispered fiercely. "I'll take care of you."

She just didn't know how she was going to do that.

She stared out of the window, her heart throbbing within her, and her eye caught on a boy standing on the edge of the street... a pale boy, very thin, with a tray around his neck.

Juliette gasped. She scrubbed at the window with her sleeve again and pressed her nose to the cold glass, certain that her eyes had deceived her. But they had not.

It was Emory. He looked weak and pale, but she knew his eyes instantly as they scanned over the front of the building, searching, as always, for her window. Juliette pressed both hands to the window, but she couldn't open it; it had been painted shut years ago.

She glanced at Reuben again. He was still sound asleep, and she couldn't stop herself. She turned and hurried out of the tenement; her feet as quiet as she could make them. She jogged past all the closed doors and trotted down the long slant of the staircase. Her heart was thudding in her mouth as she reached the front door, praying he would still be there.

When Juliette pressed her hand to the doorknob, she hesitated. There were so many dangers out there. The red-eyed shadow loomed as always, but more than that, the whooping cough that had now taken both parents from her had also come from somewhere out there. She froze on the threshold, her heart fluttering, but Emory was the only person she could think of who might be able to help her and Reuben. He was the only thing that might make her smile right now.

She shoved the door open and stumbled into the street all at once. The cold snatched instantly at her breath, and faint droplets prickled on her skin, bitterly cold. Ignoring both, Juliette scanned the street in front of her frantically, searching for Emory.

He had his back to her when she saw him, and he was melting into the crowd, giving up and leaving.

"Emory!" she cried out. "Emory, wait!"

For a heart-wrenching moment, she thought he couldn't hear her over the hubbub of conversation, but then he stopped and looked left and right.

Juliette picked her way forward, looking around nervously to avoid the traffic. "Emory," she called again.

The back of her neck prickled, and she wheeled around. Was the red-eyed shadow behind her? She saw nothing, but chills scampered up and down her spine like mice.

"Juliette."

Emory's voice cut through her fear like a sunbeam through clouds. She spun, and he was pushing his way across the street toward her, smiling that crooked smile. He was so thin, and his hair was limp and dirty, but the smile was exactly the same as it had always been.

"Emory, you're alive," she cried.

Emory's smile faded. "Juliette, what are you doing out here?" he gasped as he reached her.

Juliette's eyes filled with tears. "I saw you from the window." She pointed. "That's my window."

"But why did you come out here?" Emory gasped. "It's not safe. The whooping cough is everywhere. It—" He stopped and shuddered. "It nearly killed me."

"It's in the building, too," said Juliette. Tears spilled over. "It took Mama."

"Oh, Juliette." Emory's mouth drooped. "I'm so sorry. And Reuben? Is he—"

"He's fine," said Juliette hastily. "He's completely fine."

"Oh... good." Emory blew out a breath. "I'm glad to hear that." He reached out and squeezed her hand. "I'm sorry about your mama."

"I don't know what to do." Juliette bit back a sob. "The rent man is going to come soon, and I have no money, Emory. Nothing. What's going to happen to us? We can't be thrown onto the streets." She couldn't hold back the sob anymore. "Reuben can't be homeless."

"We'll work something out," said Emory. "You could go begging."

"We'll never earn enough in one day," said Juliette. "Never."

"Maybe the rent man will give you a little time," said Emory.

Juliette thought of the sallow-faced man and his cruel, cruel eyes. "I don't think so." She covered her face with her hands. "Emory, we're going to die."

"No, you're not." Emory squeezed her hand. "We're not going to let that happen."

Juliette stared up at him. "I thought that about Mama," she whispered, "and it still happened. She still died. She's still gone."

"That's different," said Emory.

Juliette didn't see how. She pressed both hands to her mouth, feeling hot tears run over her fingers, turning frigid by the time they reached her pinkies with the cold wind blowing over them.

"What about the nice lady who's been teaching you to read?" Emory asked. "Margie, isn't it?"

Juliette glanced back at the building. "What about her?"

"She might help you," said Emory. "Maybe you could stay with her if you found a job and Reuben helped with begging. Then you could help to pay for her rent."

Juliette bit the inside of her cheek. "I don't know. Her husband... he doesn't like us."

Emory sighed. "If there's one thing I know about cruel men, it's that they like money, even if they don't like children."

Juliette nodded. "I... I'll ask her," she said.

She would have to. Margie was now her only hope.

PART II

CHAPTER 8

Two Years Later

DUST hung thick in the air of the cotton mill. It had settled over Juliette's hands, thick and crusty; it stung her eyes, and with every breath she took, she could feel it tickling her nose and throat and chest. She felt a sneeze gathering in the back of her nose, but before it could come out, she heard it: the distant, faint *snap* of breaking thread.

Juliette spun to the right. The great cotton mule clacked and rattled before her, the length of the entire room, dozens of rough threads of white cotton hissing and whirling as it spun. Each line was straight and taut, but ten feet away, one trailed hopelessly in the air.

Juliette sprang forward, but she was already too late.

"YOU," the overseer bellowed from the corner of the room. "Hurry up."

Juliette's heart leapt into her mouth. She darted over to the broken thread, grabbed the ends and tied them together as quickly as she could. The rough thread snagged on her calluses and stung her fingers, but in seconds, the knot was tied, and the mule spun forth, unimpeded.

Heart racing, Juliette looked up. The overseer was a short man, with a bulbous, scarlet nose and little piggy eyes. They were glaring at Juliette now as he stormed to her.

"What was *that?*" the overseer shrieked.

Juliette cowered.

"How *can* you be so slow?" the overseer demanded. "Your work is easy. You have so little to do, and yet you can't even get this right."

"I'm sorry, sir," Juliette whimpered.

"I don't care if you're sorry. Don't let it happen again," the overseer hissed. His rotten breath huffed in Juliette's face, and she closed her eyes, trembling, braced for a blow. But he was in a good mood today. He turned and strode away, and Juliette exhaled slowly.

The pressure built behind her nose. She tried to stop it, but the sneeze was loud and explosive, and it stopped the overseer dead in his tracks.

He whipped around. "What was that, child?"

"Nothing, sir." Juliette dragged her sleeve over her nose. "Nothing at all."

His eyes narrowed. "Are you sick?"

Juliette's heart thumped in her chest. It was the same question she asked herself every night as she trudged home though the cold, panting as she climbed the last hill before the tenement building.

"No, sir," she whispered.

The overseer leaned closer to her, studying her like she was a faulty mechanism in the cotton mule. She forced herself to breathe slowly.

"No one gets better," he hissed in her face. "No one with brown lung *ever* gets better."

Juliette didn't know if that was true, but she'd seen many coughing, pale children leave this factory. None of them had ever come back.

"Pray you don't have it," the overseer snarled. He shrugged. "But if you do, at least there are plenty of other worthless scraps like you on the streets."

He stalked away, and Juliette muffled her next sneeze with her sleeve. Was she about to cough? She heard the echo of her mother's terrible, struggling breaths in the back of her mind, remembering that awful whooping noise that filled the tenement on that dreadful winter two years ago now, and pushed the memory away.

She didn't have the luxury of dying. She had to take care of Reuben.

When the next thread snapped, Juliette was upon it in seconds.

❧

I⊤ was long past dark when Juliette plodded up the muddy street. There were no carts or donkeys here now, no foot traffic coming from up ahead; only the tired trickle of workers making their way home from the factory district twenty minutes' walk behind Juliette. The familiar outline of the windows of her building, firelight flickering dimly behind them, beckoned her to urge her aching feet just a little faster.

"No, no. Leave me alone."

The high, panicked voice made Juliette's blood freeze. Her head snapped up to where two large figures loomed over the tiny shape of Reuben, cowering on the pavement.

"It's mine," he sobbed, clutching his hand to his chest. "It's mine."

One of the bigger boys grabbed his arm. "Stop that, or I'll break your arm."

Reuben struggled. With his free hand, he swung a tiny fist wildly into the boy's chest. The blow was puny and pathetic, and the other boy seized his arm and twisted. Reuben screamed.

Juliette was upon them before they knew what was happening. "That's my *brother*," she shrieked. She kicked the first boy in the shins so hard that he screamed, then slammed her fist painfully into the other boy's cheek. He stumbled back, shocked, and before he could gather himself, Juliette seized her brother's hand.

"Run, Roo," she cried.

They bolted across the street, dodging curses and kicks as they bumped into tired workers. Juliette didn't look back to see if the boys were behind them. She didn't slow down until she'd shoved the door open and hauled Reuben into the building behind her.

"Juli—" Reuben began.

"Run," Julie snapped. She slammed the door shut and shoved him, hard, in the direction of the stairs.

They scrambled up the stairs together and only stopped when they reached the landing on the third floor. Juliette clutched her brother's arm, digging her fingernails into his threadbare coat, and listened. She could hear nothing except the rush of breath in her lungs and felt a faint pang of hope. Maybe she didn't have brown lung after all.

"I think they're gone," said Reuben.

Hot fury lanced through Juliette's belly. She whirled to face him. "What were you doing?"

Reuben shrank back. "I'm sorry, Juli. I thought some of the workers might give me something."

"I told you never to be out begging after dark," Juliette snapped.

"I just wanted to help." Tears filled Reuben's eyes. "You always come home after dark."

"I don't have a choice. You do," said Juliette. "And you're going to stay in the tenement anytime when it's dark, all right?"

Reuben blinked back the tears and clenched his jaw. "You can't tell me what to do."

"Yes, I can," said Juliette.

"You're not Mama," Reuben shot back.

Pain stabbed through her heart. She gripped his arm tighter. "Mama's not here," she yelled.

The tears returned. Reuben ripped his arm from her grasp and ran down the hall, sobbing.

Juliette sighed. "Roo!"

He ignored her. Pushing open Margie's door, he rushed into the tenement.

Shoulders slumped, Juliette dragged herself into the tiny room. It was spotless, as usual, but only a little less bare than it used to be two years ago. Across the room from the sleeping pallet, wedged tightly into the corner, there was a new sleeping mat. Reuben was curled up on it, fists pressed into his eyes, sobbing. Margie knelt beside him.

"Juli?" Margie looked up. Her cheeks were more pinched than ever these days. "What happened?"

"I told him not to go begging after dark." Juliette flung herself down on the corner of the mat, finally resting her aching feet.

"I just wanted to help," Reuben sobbed.

"There, there, Roo." Margie rubbed his back. "I know you did. But Juli's right. It's not safe."

Reuben sobbed harder. Juliette leaned her head against the rickety wooden wall and closed her eyes, far too tired for this.

"Come now, Roo," said Margie. "Show us what you got today."

Reuben sat up, brightening. He held out a hand and tipped two tiny coins into Margie's palm. Both were pennies.

"Tuppence?" Juliette cried.

Margie shot her a look and smiled. "Tuppence. That's lovely. We'll buy some bread tomorrow."

"I'm hungry," said Reuben.

"Of course, you are." Margie got up and bustled to the rickety yet spotless little cast-iron stove in the corner. "There's soup."

Juliette was silent as Margie spooned up small helpings of bone broth into chipped enamel bowls. The children ate quietly; the broth was hot, but it tasted like little more than water with a few wilted bits of vegetables in it. Juliette tried to make it last as long as she could, but her thoughts were filled with Reuben.

He'd risked his life for tuppence. *Tuppence.* Had Londoners' hearts grown harder in the past two years, or did they simply no longer consider Reuben beautiful enough to give him sixpence at a time, as they once did? Juliette glanced sideways at her brother, his skinny limbs, his mop of hair. He looked as perfect as ever in her eyes.

A familiar, heavy tread sounded on the landing.

Margie's eyes widened. "Quick. Give me those bowls."

The children slurped the last of their soup and handed Margie the bowls and spoons. She hastily rinsed them, her usual care forgotten in her rush, and dried them on a rag before setting them out on the wooden box she and Bert used for eating.

The footsteps were at the door.

"Remember," Margie whispered, and laid a finger on her lips.

Juliette wrapped Reuben in her arms and tugged him down on the sleeping mat. She pulled their thin blanket over them just in time as the door creaked open.

"Bertie, darling," Margie cried. Her voice was forced and brittle, nothing like the warm tones she used to greet Juliette and Reuben.

"Is there food?" Bert grunted. His voice was lower and harsher than it used to be, and so was he.

"Of course, dear. Lovely soup," said Margie.

A ladle clattered on the bowls as Margie served soup with shaking hands.

"What is this, woman?" Bert growled.

Margie swallowed audibly. "It's bone broth, dear."

"Where's the meat?"

"There—there are only bones, darling. It's rent day in two days. I thought we'd better save the money."

"I know where the meat's gone." Bert's voice lowered. "You've given it to the two urchins."

"Of course not, pet. I told you," Margie blurted out, "the children don't eat here. They help themselves. They're only sleeping here. And they're helping to pay for the rent, remember? Hasn't that been a big help?"

"A big help," Bert growled. "I wish I'd never let you talk me into bringing those two brats into our house."

"Oh, Bert, darling, you don't mean that," Margie quavered.

"I mean every word of it, woman. They do nothing but eat our food and get in the way," Bert snapped. "If you want children so badly, why don't you just have them?"

A sudden silence fell. Juliette's heart ached for Margie.

"How could you?" Margie whispered.

"I'm sorry, Margaret." Bert didn't sound sorry. "I just don't understand why we don't have any children."

"Neither do I," Margie whimpered, and dissolved into quiet sobbing.

Juliette listened to her weeping until sleep finally came for her.

JULIETTE'S FEET ACHED, but that was nothing compared to the sting in her heart.

Jostled by the crowd of workers as they spilled from the ugly maw of the factory, Juliette was frozen on the sidewalk. She stared down at the pitiful coins in her hand, her cheek still throbbing from the cruel slap that the overseer had dealt her when she'd asked him why her wage was so low.

"Why do you think, you stupid mite?" he'd yelled at her. "You're slow. Slow. Slow."

Tears burned Juliette's eyes. How was she going to afford her unrealistic proportion of the rent this week? She was bad at sums, but she knew full well that this would never be enough. The throb of her calves, worn out from a day sprinting up and down the length of the cotton mule, brought the cruel truth home. It didn't matter how hard she tried; they would always find a reason to dock her pay.

She sucked in a long, trembling breath and tucked the money into her pocket. There was nothing she could do about it now. Perhaps she would think of something on the long walk home.

A quiet rumble of thunder in the sky matched her mood as she plodded down the street, surrounded by a swarm of exhausted workers, men, women, and children. They all hung their heads and stared at nothing as they walked, saying nothing except perhaps to commiserate with one another in quiet tones. No one spoke to Juliette. They were like the cattle she saw being driven to the slaughterhouse nearby, too tired to question their fate. They dragged their exhaustion with them like oxen pulling a plow.

Like always, Juliette kept her eyes trained on the dirt in front of her, one hand in her pocket, clutched around her few coins. She had no interest in anything near her. She only wanted to get home.

Then she felt it.

The gaze of the red-eyed shadow.

Juliette sucked in a breath. It had been more than a year since the last time she had felt it, but she knew it instantly, the feeling that something was stalking her, following her. She whipped around, and a thin, sickly woman almost crashed into her.

"Out of the way!" The woman shoved her aside.

Juliette reeled, trying not to bump into anyone else. People pushed past her, dead-eyed and impervious to her terror. Her eyes swept across the crowd, searching for whatever was following her.

"Where are you?" she whispered, shaking. "What do you want with me?"

Reuben... She had to get home to Reuben.

She spun around, and her eye caught a familiar figure strolling down the pavement across the street.

Bert.

For a confused moment, she thought he was the malevolent presence she felt, that Bert and the red-eyed shadow were one and the same. But it couldn't be. Bert was strolling in the along a ways off, and for once, he wasn't scowling. Instead, he moved with an easy, rolling stride; his head was high, and he was smiling. There was even a wilted little wildflower in his buttonhole.

Where was he going?

Workers jostled her, but Juliette ignored them, rooted to the spot. They had left the factory district behind and come to the tenement buildings on the outskirts of Whitechapel, and Bert now strode up to one of these. It was somewhat nicer than the building where Juliette lived; this one had sturdy brick walls, and many of the windows still had some glass in them, even though some had sacking for curtains.

Bert took out a key and unlocked the front door, then let himself into the building. Juliette could hear him whistling a jaunty sea-shanty as he shut the door behind him. She hardly knew why, but she drifted much nearer and stood on the pavement, listening to the clump of Bert's feet on stairs that sounded solid.

There was a knock, and movement in one of the second-floor windows. A woman strode past the window. She was ravishingly pretty, her hair raven-dark, and her belly curved with promise. When she opened the door, her smile made her even prettier.

Bert stepped into the tenement, and Juliette's breath caught in her throat. She knew little of these things, but every fiber of her body was telling her that something was wrong.

Bert's smile widened. The woman gripped his hands, and he pulled her close and kissed her, long and tenderly, in a way that Juliette had never seen him kiss Margie. She gasped and clapped her hands to her mouth.

After several long, long moments, during which Bert's hands roved over the woman's body, they broke apart. Bert said something, and the woman laughed. She turned to the window and her eyes met Juliette's.

Fear panged down to Juliette's toes, but she didn't stir. She simply stared at the woman, open-mouthed, her heart racing.

The woman frowned and said something to Bert. Before Juliette could move, he came to the window, and the instant that his eyes lit upon her, she knew she was in terrible danger. The look on his face restarted her heart. Panic surged through her body, and Juliette turned and bolted.

There was a yell behind her and the crash of a slamming door. "Stop that girl," Bert bellowed. "Stop her!"

Juliette tripled her pace. Weaving and ducking through the plodding herd of workers, she ran for all she was worth. Her sore feet in her holey shoes slammed against the cobblestones, and air rushed in her lungs until she felt they would explode, but she didn't slow down. Even when hands grasped at her, even when feet stuck out to trip her, she tore herself free, hurdled every obstacle, put her head down and kept running.

Nothing could stop her. Not when Reuben needed her, and she didn't know what Bert would do if he laid his hands on her.

She didn't know when Bert stopped chasing her. All she knew was that she reached home in one piece, raced up the steps, and fell sobbing into Margie's lap. And though Margie begged to know what had happened, all Juliette did was sob.

❧

When Bert's heavy footsteps clumped on the hallway that evening, Juliette's intestines tied themselves into knots.

She curled herself more tightly around Reuben, pretending to be asleep, as they always did when Bert came home. But tonight, she wondered where he was coming home from. When Margie asked about Bert's low wages, he always said that that was a dockworker's lot, that the bosses were cruel, that they looked for reasons to cut his pay. Juliette had always believed him.

Until now.

Did he even go to the docks? It seemed unlikely. Where had he met that woman?

Who was the father of her unborn baby?

Juliette squeezed Reuben so tight that he grunted. She forced herself to release him slightly so that Bert wouldn't know she was awake.

She had expected the atmosphere between Bert and Margie to be cold and brittle, like frosted glass. Instead, he was more cheerful than normal. He didn't mention the children. He didn't mention money. He even laughed once, and Juliette's heart bled when she heard Margie laugh in return, surprised but delighted.

She finally began to think that nothing would ever come of it, that maybe she'd imagined some stranger as Bert, and sleep stole slowly over her exhausted soul. It was abruptly banished much later when Bert's hand wrapped around her arm, and she was plucked from the sleeping mat and hauled out of the door. She opened her mouth to scream, but Bert's huge hand clapped over it, stopping her.

"Shut up," he snarled. "Shut up."

It was very dark. Juliette didn't know how long she'd been asleep. The only light came from the streetlamp outside the window, casting a dim glow into the hallway. There was no sound from inside the tenement; Margie and Reuben must both still be asleep.

"If you scream, I'll kill you," Bert hissed.

Juliette's blood raced. She believed every word he said.

"Do you understand?" said Bert.

Trembling, Juliette nodded.

The hand vanished from her mouth. Bert grabbed her by the shoulders and spun her around to face him, and his eyes were bloodshot. A fruity stench rolled from his breath, the way it often did when he got home from work.

"I never wanted you here," he said. "I only did it because I thought, if there were children, then maybe Margie would—" He stopped. "That's none of your business."

Juliette swallowed. His hands were two vice grips on her arms.

"You're a pest," he growled. "You've been in my way since the beginning. I never want to see you again." He pushed her away from him. "Take your brother and go."

Juliette's heart stuttered in her chest. "But—"

Bert's eyes were two malevolent blood moons glaring down at her in the darkness. "Go."

"Wh–where?" Juliette sobbed. "We have nowhere to go. We'd be on the streets. How will we survive the winter?"

"You're not *my* children. Your own useless parents should have cared for you. Would have, if they'd wanted you," Bert hissed.

"My parents are dead," Juliette cried.

Bert's eyes narrowed. Juliette forced herself to lower her breath. "Please, sir. Please. Let us stay. We're helping with the rent. We're paying for our food. Please—"

"Take the boy and go or I'll snatch him from his bed and fling him into the cold myself," Bert hissed.

Juliette's heart shrivelled within her at the thought of Reuben, her poor, sweet Reuben, being dragged so forcibly from comparative warmth and cast out into the frosty street. A cold wind howled around the building, and Juliette shivered where she stood. What would happen then? She'd seen the street children, their hollow eyes, their missing toes and fingers. She'd heard them crying sometimes when she passed them on her way home from the factory.

Something flared within her at the thought of Reuben in that state. It couldn't happen. She couldn't let it.

"I said—" Bert began.

Juliette stepped forward. The words spilled out of her. "If you throw Reuben and me out, I'll tell Margie."

Bert's jaw snapped shut. "*What?*"

"I said what I said." Juliette raised her chin, unsure whether she was being reckless with courage or with terror. "I saw you with that woman. Is that your baby?"

Bert's eyes filled with fury. He drew back a hand to strike her, and Juliette cowered, but the words kept coming.

"Margie doesn't have to know," she choked out. "She never needs to know. I'll never tell unless you cast us onto the streets."

Bert's hand stopped. "You wouldn't come back here," he snarled. "Not if I throw you out."

"You can't visit that lady *and* stand guard over Margie all the time," Juliette spat. "We'll sneak back. I'll find a way. Margie will know... but not if you let us stay." She prayed for forgiveness, knowing that she should tell Margie anyway—but which was more important—honesty, or her brother's very life? "If you let us stay, I'll never say a thing."

Bert's jaw worked, his teeth grinding audibly. Slowly, he lowered his hand.

"Fine," he snarled. "But tread carefully, child." He leaned closer. "You can't tell anyone anything if you're dead."

He turned and staggered back into the tenement.

Juliette stood in the hallway, feeling as though a chill wind had just blown all the way through her. Surely... surely Bert didn't mean it. Surely those last words were simply the drunken ravings of a fool.

Juliette swallowed hard. She would still have to sleep with one eye open.

CHAPTER 9

EVERY SUNDAY, Juliette woke with a slightly lighter feeling in her chest.

She knew it was Sunday even before she opened her eyes because of the quiet in the tenement. Throughout the building, people rested instead of hurrying to the difficult jobs that paid them tiny scraps of wages. Sometimes, Bert would still be on the pallet, snoring beside Margie.

But not today; not for the last few Sundays, in fact. Ever since Juliette had seen him with that woman, Bert had taken to disappearing more nights than he stayed. It suited her well enough, except for Sunday nights, when she waited and waited for him to come home. He always returned drunk and angry and yelling, but at least he returned with rent money.

That was a worry for this evening, though. Now, Juliette's eyes fluttered slowly open to see a shaft of golden sunlight falling into the tenement. Margie was lying with her back to the children, her breaths slow and deep. Reuben was in Juliette's arms. A golden curl lay on his cheek, shining softly in the sun.

Juliette sat up and shook him softly. "Come on, Roo. Let's go for something to eat." For once, her pay had not been docked yesterday. She could afford breakfast as well as supper today.

Reuben sat up, instantly wide awake, and Margie stirred feebly on the pallet.

"Food?" Reuben jumped to his feet.

Margie rolled over, groggy and pale. "There isn't any," she mumbled. She began to sit up, then winced and pressed a hand to her side before sagging back onto the pallet.

"Hush, Margie. Don't move," said Juliette. "We're going to get some, once we've had some tea."

There were a few leaves left in the bottom of the tin, and Juliette brewed them each a weak cup with no milk or sugar. The fluid tasted little better than muddy water, but it was hot at least, and they drank quietly. Juliette burned her lips a little in her haste.

"Come on." She grabbed Reuben's arm while Margie was only halfway through her cup. "Let's go."

Reuben giggled and skipped, sensing his sister's high energy, as they clattered down the stairs and into the street. Despite the snow that sparkled everywhere, sunlight poured from the bright blue sky, turning the world into a wonderland. There were children everywhere: some blue-faced and shivering in their threadbare clothes, some plumply bundled up in scarves and hats, but all of them were playing. Snowballs flew, and laughter filled the air.

The day felt on the outside the way Juliette felt on the inside, and sunshine poured through her soul when they reached the market square, and her eyes flew immediately to Emory's corner. He was right there, as he always was, with his tray around his neck. His hair had grown; it tickled his shoulders now, and the tips were nearly blond, bleached by constant exposure. It was a better day for him today than it had been of late; there was a small pile of rags on his tray, alongside a few pieces of white-bleached bone.

Juliette waved to him, her grip tightening on Reuben's hand, and hurried across the market square.

"Hi, Emory," she called.

He turned, and her heart panged at the sight of how his shoulders jutted against the same threadbare coat he'd been wearing for the past two years. It no longer closed all the way around his chest, and he'd tied it in place with a bit of grubby string.

"Juliette." Emory beamed. "It's so good to see you." Despite his thin cheeks, his smile was still as jaunty as ever.

"How are you?" Juliette asked.

The smile didn't flicker. "I'm all right. In fact, I might even have a job."

"A job?" Juliette cried. Her heart stuttered within her. She tried not to imagine an overseer screaming at Emory, beating him if he made tiny mistakes. Then again, how many people screamed at him and beat him here on these very streets?

"Yes. I've heard there's a rat-catcher looking for a new boy," said Emory.

What happened to the old one? Juliette wondered, but she didn't ask. She'd seen the rat-catcher prowling the streets here. He was a long, thin, pale, bony man who never smiled.

"He pays ha'penny a rat. That means that if I catch a lot of rats, I could eat three meals a day. Or even find a tenement again." Emory beamed.

"That's—that's good news," said Juliette, not sure that it was, but unwilling to quench his smile.

A woman in a ragged dress strayed past, her eyes lingering on Emory's tray. He stepped forward and raised his voice. "Rags and bones. Lovely and clean—I washed them myself." His dirty fingernails dug into the tray as his hands trembled. "A penny for them all."

The woman slowed, shuddered, and then hurried away. Emory let out a quiet sigh but pasted his smile back on before he turned to Juliette.

"How about you?" he asked. "How are you?"

The words balanced on the tip of Juliette's tongue. *Margie's sick, again, and tomorrow I have to leave Reuben all on his own with her again. I don't know if he'll be able to give her water when she needs it. I don't know if she'll get better or worse. Bert pays the rent, but I don't know for how long. I don't know if he's going to come and get me someday for what I saw and said. And the overseer at the factory hates me, and there's a new draft from the back wall of our tenement, and when Bert does come home, he always shouts and throws things and last time he threw a fork right at me and I just don't know what to do—*

She took a deep breath, all of her worries crushing her lungs, and then felt the pressure of Reuben's eyes on her. They were huge and scared, and she realized that her eyes were filling with tears.

Juliette's grip on his hand tightened, and she blinked them back. "Fine," she said. "Just fine."

Emory's eyes searched hers, and she longed to tell him everything. But she couldn't let Reuben know what she'd seen or how afraid she was or about the red-eyed shadow that still sometimes dogged her on her way home from work.

"Why don't you tell us a story?" she managed.

"The story about the rabbits," said Reuben instantly.

Emory's crooked smile returned. "Well, all right, then."

Reuben mouthed the words along with him as he began. "Once upon a time, there were three little rabbits..."

⁂

EMORY COCKED his cap at a cheerful angle as he strolled down the street, running through the directions that the flower-girl at the market square had given him. She was the one who had found out about the boy who had died falling into the sewer while trying to catch rats, and she had told Emory about the rat-catcher looking for someone new.

"Go down the long street to the crossroads," she'd explained. "Turn left at the abandoned factory, then go down two blocks, turn right, and go to the building next to the one that's all burned up."

Emory had thanked her and wished he had tuppence or anything to give her. Instead, he'd lain silently on his newspaper bedding in the alley behind the tanner's all night, smelling the reek of curing leather, and dreaming of a day when he would go to sleep with a full belly for two nights in a row. Perhaps even more.

He turned down the street that the girl had told him and instantly spotted the warehouse that had been gutted by fire. It looked as though it had been standing there for years, forgotten by the world, brick beginning to show through the soot as snow and rain and smog had washed the black away. Its walls were jagged and uneven, the roof long gone except for a few blackened struts, and a pile of hopeless rubble lay where its floor used to be.

Emory pushed past it and reached the building where he would find the rat-catcher. It was a great, hollow warehouse that looked completely abandoned. Someone had scribbled an ugly word over the walls with a stick of charcoal; it would wash away, but now it stood there, spartan and disgusting. Emory couldn't read, but he recognized the shape of it. There was no glass in any of the windows, and they were plugged with planks and bits of newspaper.

He would have thought that this was the wrong place if it hadn't been for the shouting.

"Two? Two?" It was a male voice, high-pitched and nasal. "You bring me *two* and expect a penny?"

"Sir," a feeble voice replied, "you said—"

There was a meaty thud; the sound of a slap. A boy's voice started crying.

"Ha'penny is all you'll have," the man snarled. "And that's final."

Emory swallowed hard. He'd received his share of blows from the harsh men and women of London's streets, but was this going to be worse? What if he was leaving the frying-pan to fall into the fire?

He stepped back, ready to flee back to his street corner and his tray, but then he saw Juliette in his mind's eye. He saw the tortured terror on her face, the tears that shone in her eyes, the way her lips trembled with the weight of everything that she couldn't tell him. He didn't know what was happening in Juliette's life, but he knew that she was unhappy and scared. Emory longed to help her with everything in his soul.

He took a deep breath and squared his shoulders. He couldn't do anything for her if he couldn't even feed himself.

"For you, Juli," he whispered, and pushed the door open.

The stench that rose from within was a stomach-turning mixture of the sickly sweet smell of decay mixed with the salty, metallic tang of blood. Only a dim portion of faded sunlight made its way into the warehouse from the gaps and chinks in the ruined roof. Dust and dirt hung in the air, and through it, Emory could see the silhouettes of a long, thin man and two cowering boys. One had his hands covering his face.

"Stop that blubbering," the man ordered.

The boy stopped. His companion, a lanky fellow, held out two very small rats, their tails clenched between his fingers. They were dead, their tiny claws tucked against their bodies.

The rat-catcher snatched them and tossed a penny to the lanky boy. "Get out of my sight," he snapped. "And do better next time."

The boys fled. Emory stepped aside to clear their path to the door. His foot crunched on something soft and furry, and he gasped and sprang back. As his eyes adjusted to the light, he realized that the floor wasn't covered in dirt.

It was covered in dead rats.

They were laid out in neat rows on the floor, nose-to-tail, big and small, fat and thin. Their terrible long yellow teeth shone in the faint sunlight. Their bodies, motionless and furry, looked like discarded bits of fluff, too insubstantial to be alive. Their tails were stiff and curled with death. Many had holes blown in them with bullets or knives, and almost all of them had crushed skulls, eyeballs mashed into fragments of bone.

Nausea roiled in Emory's gut. He stumbled back a step.

"What do you want?" the rat-catcher demanded, his voice echoing hollowly in the large, dim space.

Emory sucked in a long, frightened breath. *Juliette*, he reminded himself. *Think of little Juliette.*

He stepped forward. "I want to catch rats." His voice sounded stronger than it felt.

The rat-catcher tilted his head to one side. He wore a flat-topped hat with a tattered brim, and it shadowed his eyes so that Emory could only see the cruel curve of his smile.

"You think so, do you, boy?" he hissed. "Have you ever been down in a sewer, among the stink and the filth? Have you seen them swarming down a narrow tunnel toward you? Have you heard the scrabble of their tiny claws on the bricks as they get closer... and closer... and closer?"

With every word, the rat-catcher came nearer, until Emory could see his yellow eyes and smell his rotten breath. He stood his ground with all of his might.

"Have you ever grabbed something living and squirming with your bare hand, boy?" the rat-catcher hissed. "Have you ever gripped a living thing and crushed it to death with your fingers?"

Emory's heart thundered, but he met the rat-catcher's eyes as boldly as he dared.

"I've slept on the streets and woken with rat bites on my feet," he said. "And I've chased them away from bits of food so that I could grab it. I think I know them quite well enough."

The rat-catcher's eyes narrowed. "You do, do you?"

Emory didn't know what to say. He was trembling, but he stood his ground as boldly as he could.

"All right then, boy," the rat-catcher muttered. "You look altogether too small and skinny to last more'n a month to me, but do you know how many rats I need to catch?"

Emory swallowed. "As—as many as it takes to keep the streets clean?"

"Thirteen a day," the rat-catcher snarled. "Five thousand a year. Why, when I catch that many, the queen herself will feather my nest." He smirked horribly. "Can you catch that many rats, child?"

"Yes," Emory whimpered, not knowing if it was true. "I can."

"I hope so." The rat-catcher folded his arms. "Ha'penny each, but don't bring me two or three. Bring me five or six. Or thirteen."

"Yes, sir," said Emory.

"Good." The rat-catcher plucked something from his pocket and held it out. "I'm a good man with a good heart, boy, so I'll start you off with a little of this."

It was a tiny bottle, hardly big enough to hold more than a few drops. Emory took it. "What is it?" he asked. "Poison?"

The rat-catcher chuckled. "Poison? No, boy. It's oil. Smells sweet. The rats love it."

Emory stared at him.

"You rub it on your hands," said the rat-catcher. "Then they'll come right up to you, wanting to take a bite out of you."

Emory swallowed. "And then... I catch them?"

"Yes," said the rat-catcher.

"But... how do I do that without getting bitten?" Emory asked.

The rat-catcher held up his hands, and Emory's breath hitched. The scars were not the worst of it, although they were awful, pink and puckered. The half-healed wounds scared him, flesh showing, scabby chunks all over the palms and fingers.

"You don't," the rat catcher sneered.

It took everything in Emory's spirit not to turn and run for his life. He stumbled back a step with a cry of fear, but somehow, he didn't run.

"I'll be back," he croaked. "With rats."

The rat-catcher chuckled. "You had better."

CHAPTER 10

As Juliette dragged her tired limbs up the stairs after yet another day of endless work, she could hear Reuben's weeping.

She stopped on the top step, heart thudding, and listening. Reuben's crying was nothing new. For the last week—ever since Margie had stopped wanting to eat—he had sobbed every time Juliette got home, tired little sobs, tears rolling down a dirty, pale face, as though he'd been crying a long time.

It was heart-wrenching, but now, Juliette listened intently. There were worse things than caring for Margie all day.

Like losing her.

The sobs were small and quiet, though, and Juliette let out a breath. Surely, Margie was still alive.

She plodded up to the tenement and pushed the door open. "I brought fish," she called, holding it up.

Reuben lifted his head, and Juliette's heart skipped a beat. He wasn't curled on the sleeping mat; instead, he sat in Margie's lap, his little head resting on her chest. She was pale and breathing hard, her lips edged with blue, but she was sitting up for the first time in days. Her eyes lit up when Juliette came in.

"Juli, darling," she said. "Come in, come in."

Juliette closed the door beside her and hurried over to them. "Margie, you look so much better." When she touched Margie's forehead, it was dry and cool.

"I *am* much better, thanks to this little angel." Margie hugged Reuben. "He bathed my forehead all day, didn't you?"

Reuben smiled, and Juliette realized that his tears were of relief. She decided not to tell Margie that he'd been spending all day bathing her forehead for a full week. When she got home, Juliette would take over, and keep going until she fell asleep from sheer exhaustion.

"I've brought fish," Juliette said. "Do you want some, Margie?"

Margie's eyes lit up. "Yes, please."

Juliette unfolded the paper and scooped the fish onto a tin plate. The fishmonger had been tired and ready to go home;

she'd been lucky to buy a whole fish, and it barely even smelled sour at all.

She set the plate down on the pallet in front of Margie, and took tiny bites so that she could have the pleasure of watching Margie tear open the white fish and gulp down great, hungry bites. Her thin ribs and shoulders shuddered as she ate, and she didn't stop until it was all gone. Reuben's mouth was smeared with fat from the fish; he sucked his lips carefully, getting every drop of oil.

"Ah, Juli, thank you," said Margie. "That was wonderful."

"I'll bring bread tomorrow," said Juliette.

Reuben cuddled down close to Margie. "I'm glad you're better," he whispered.

Margie stroked his hair. "Where's Bert?"

"I don't know," said Juliette. "He must be—working tonight."

Margie looked away and closed her eyes, leaning her head back against the wall. Her thin fingers tangled with Reuben's thick, golden locks.

"My brother said this would happen, you know," she murmured.

Juliette curled up next to Margie. "Your brother who lived in the country?"

"Yes," said Margie. "The one who looked after the sheep."

"He chased a fox away from the flock with a stone and a sling once," Reuben murmured sleepily. "He took the baby lamb right out of the fox's mouth and saved it."

"Exactly." Margie chuckled softly. "The very same."

"What do you mean, he said this would happen?" Juliette asked.

Margie shook her head. "Never mind, poppet. I should never have said anything. It's all a silly, grownup matter to you, in any case."

Juliette glanced at Reuben. The little boy's eyes were closed, and he took slow, even breaths.

"I want to know," she said, leaning against Margie. "Please tell me."

"Poor mite." Margie wrapped an arm around Juliette's shoulders. "I suppose I'm the silly one, telling you that it's a grownup matter, when you're the one who works every day like a Trojan to feed us."

Juliette closed her eyes. "Tell me about your brother," she whispered. "And the house in the country. Why did you ever leave all those animals and the sunrises and the smells you tell us about?"

"Because I was a fool," said Margie softly.

She took a few deep breaths, and Juliette waited, her head resting on Margie's chest. Her breaths made crackly, rattling sounds, but the lub-dub of her heart was warm and familiar.

"His name is Ralph," said Margie. "Ralph Mills. He was a sweet, silly, naughty little boy who grew up into a big, kind, silly man. I loved him very much, but I think he loved me more. I don't know that anyone has ever loved me the way he did."

"When was the last time you saw him?" Juliette asked.

"Years ago now, pet. *Years*." Margie sighed. "He must be grey by now. He's nearly ten years older than me, you know. Maybe that's why he always loved me so much. I was his baby sister. By the time I was five he used to carry me around on his hip and help me to feed the little lambs. I loved it."

"What about your mama and papa?" Juliette asked. "What were they like?"

"Lovely," said Margie. "Harsh in their way, but kind. They were strict, but they loved us both dearly, and they worked hard so that we could have a good life on the farm." She sighed.

Juliette wondered why anyone would walk away from a home in the country with animals and people who loved you and enough food. She wanted to ask, but Margie's face twitched with sorrow, and her eyes were filled with tears.

"They warned me about Bert," Margie whispered.

Juliette had never heard this part of the story before. She looked up at her. "What do you mean?"

"Bert... oh, Bert." Margie wiped her eyes. "He fought in the war against the Russians, you know. It was terrible. That's why he drinks, to forget it."

"I didn't know," said Juliette.

"It broke him. The doctors sent him to the country for his convalescence. That was where I met him, walking around the fields, looking lost, like he still had one foot on the battlefield. He was so... so hurt." Margie wiped her eyes. "And so handsome. I thought I could help him, you know. I thought I could save him."

Juliette wondered what the war had been like. Back when Beatrice was alive, Juliette had once asked her about the homeless men that huddled against the wall opposite their tenement. Some had missing hands or eyes or legs. A few simply stared into the middle distance, their eyes wide, as though seeing into a different world. Juliette asked what had happened to their missing limbs.

"The war, dear," Beatrice told her. "It takes everything from people."

"What about those men who just sit there staring?" Juliette asked. "They don't have arms or legs missing."

"No, darling, but I think they lost something far greater out there," said Beatrice, and when Juliette asked, she wouldn't tell her anything more.

Margie swallowed and wiped at her tears. "I was a fool, of course. When I found out about the drinking and the gambling, I should have let him be. But I still believed I could help him... I was in love, and I would hear no reason."

"You just wanted to help him," said Juliette.

"I did, poppet. But I was too proud to believe that anyone else could help him, too. So I married him." Margie sighed. "My parents promised me I would never again set foot in their house if I married 'that scoundrel', as they said. They said they would disown me."

"So they threw you out of the house?" Juliette asked.

"No, nothing like that, dear. In hindsight, I don't think they would have done it. They were just scared and trying to stop me, even if that meant they had to threaten me." Margie sighed deeply. "It was Ralph who almost changed my mind. He didn't shout or threaten. He fell on his knees and wept. He begged, sobbing, for me to stay, to forget about Bert. If only..."

She stopped, but Juliette still felt the words hanging in the air. *If only I had listened*. Margie wished she'd never come here, she realized. She wished she'd never met Reuben and Juliette.

"I'm sorry," said Juliette.

"Me too," said Margie. "I kept thinking that everything would get better once we had children. But..." She gestured at her empty belly. "I don't think I can, poppet."

"I wish we could be your children," said Juliette. "Maybe then everything would be all right with you and Bert."

"Oh, poppet." Margie hugged her. "That's not your job. It's no child's job, as a matter of fact. I could have given him ten babies and he would still have been himself." She sighed. "No, no, my dear, don't even think about that. I love you and your brother just as you are, and nothing will ever change that."

Except if you die, Juliette thought, but didn't say.

"Bert is what he is." Margie sighed. "There's nothing anyone can do about that, except the Good Lord Himself. I just wish I could turn back time and go back to my parents and never leave them." She kissed the top of Juliette's head. "But only if I could take you two with me, of course."

"Have they ever written to you?" Juliette asked.

"No, dear. Nor have I written to them. What would I say? I'd be too ashamed, after all this time." Margie closed her eyes. "No... no... there is nothing to be done. And even if there was... I wouldn't have the strength to do it."

Her breathing grew slow and rhythmic shortly after that, but Juliette lay awake for a long time, staring at nothing, thinking of the countryside and the war.

JULIETTE COULDN'T TELL Reuben about Margie's story. What good would it do? He wouldn't understand, and besides, it would only upset him.

She kept her head down against the freezing wind that knifed into her neck and sought the holes in her thin coat. One cold hand was pressed into the pocket of her coat; she clutched Reuben's with the other, and at least that one was a little warmer. Reuben huddled close to her side, and Juliette pushed through the Sunday crowds at the market square, her heart still swirling with everything Margie had told her a few nights ago.

How could anyone leave a place with warmth, food and love behind for someone like Bert? For *anyone*? But then she thought of Emory, and she thought perhaps she did understand, just a little.

Emory. Juliette raised her head as they reached the market square. He would love Margie's story, sad though it was, because of how interesting it was. For once, Juliette could be the one telling the story, and Emory could listen. And perhaps her heart would feel a few pounds lighter if she could only share what she'd heard with someone else.

But when Juliette's gaze flew across the square to the corner where he always was, there was no sign of a jaunty boy with a tray around his neck. Only an empty space where Emory used to be.

And just like that, the wind blew colder.

JULIETTE'S BREATH curled out of her mouth and nose in thick coils of pale steam. She turned her head to the side, hoping that the dampness of her breath wouldn't reach her face; it seeped into her scarf instead, adding to the frost that sparkled on the surface of the tattered garment.

She sighed. What did it matter? She was damp already, and the skies were dark and rumbling. It wouldn't be long before she was soaked to the skin, and she'd only just set out from the factory. She was going to be wet through no matter what she did.

She hung her head and plodded on. The streets were very quiet; the factory workers had left a few minutes ahead of her, because she had been too slow with the piecing twice today, and the overseer held her back to scream at her for ten minutes and deal her three agonizing blows with his cane on the palm of her hand. It still throbbed now, tucked into her pocket, and she knew she would have to hide it from Reuben if she didn't want to upset him.

She *didn't* want to upset him. Did she? It was difficult to remember how she felt about anything when she couldn't muster the energy to feel anything but tired and bereft.

A long exhale escaped her, the steam touching warmly on her face, then turning cold and damp. She tried to remember feeling happy. Surely there was still happiness in the world? It was easy to remember: four weeks ago last Sunday, standing on the market square with Emory, listening to his story about the rabbits, the one she and Reuben both loved.

But there were no more rabbit stories now. She hadn't seen Emory since.

Juliette stumbled onward, her sore hand tucked close against her. Emory had taken all the sunshine out of the world with him when he left.

She turned down an alleyway, taking a shortcut toward the tenement. It would only save her a few minutes' walking, but she would do anything to get home a little quicker and get off her feet at last. Somewhere, a church bell tolled half past ten.

Then something creaked in the alley behind her.

Juliette stumbled to a halt, then whipped around. She searched the walls for the usual suspects in alleys of this sort; the frazzled men with the staring eyes, gibbering to themselves, clutching at thin air with claw-like hands. But there was no one there.

No one, but the feeling of being watched settled over Juliette's shoulders like a cold cloak.

She bit back a scream and spun around again. The alley was empty, except for a few twists of dirty fog, drifting on the still, cold air past the alley's exit. Juliette could just make out the faint yellow gleam of a streetlamp's reflection on a manhole cover up ahead.

Juliette's heart hammered in her chest. There were nooks and crannies everywhere, rubbish bins, doorways, windows. Places for a red-eyed shadow to hide and lie in wait. To pounce.

She stumbled a step in the direction she'd come, then stopped. Hadn't it been following her? What if it knew she was going to run this way, and seized her?

She knew it was there. She could feel it in her bones.

Her breaths came fast and raggedly. She didn't know which way to run. The red-eyed shadow was all around her, and it was closing in, crushing the breath from her lungs, making her heart thunder wildly out of control—

The manhole cover moved.

Juliette sprang back with a scream. A dreadful sound came from beneath the manhole cover, accompanying its scraping as it twitched this way, then that. The sound was a high-pitched squeaking, like the sound a tiny child would make if you shrank them and stuffed them into a glass bottle. It was a fingernails-on-glass sound.

There was a thud, and the sound stopped.

Juliette was rooted to the ground. She longed to run, but she couldn't move.

Then the manhole cover slid aside, and a grubby, pale-faced apparition climbed out of it. The thing was tall and thin, and it carried a canvas bag over one shoulder, stained and ugly and speckled with something red. The apparition's hair stood out in dirty, stiff spikes, and it was only when it turned to slide the manhole cover back into place that Juliette recognized it.

"E–E–Emory?" she stammered.

He turned, and the streetlight fell on his dirty face. His hair was caked with nameless filth, but when he smiled, it was the same smile as always.

"Juliette," he cried. "I hoped I would see you."

"What are you doing in the sewers?" Juliette gasped.

Emory patted the bag over his shoulders. "Catching rats. And hoping to find you. You said you were working for the cotton mill here, so I thought, well, if I'm catching rats at night, I might as well catch them here." His smile slipped, but he shoved it back into place. "I hoped I would find you."

"Oh, Emory." Juliette laughed with joy. The red-eyed shadow hadn't been here after all; it was just her friend. She rushed over to him, then recoiled at the stench that rolled from his body.

"Oh, sorry. The sewers don't smell good." Emory pulled a face. "Are you walking home? It's so late. Let me walk with you."

Juliette didn't like the thought of the bag full of dead rats bumping its way along with them, but she said nothing. She fell into step beside Emory as they emerged from the alley, turned left and headed for the tenement.

"What about you?" she asked. "Aren't we going out of your way?"

"Not really," said Emory. "We sleep in an abandoned building in the warehouse district, on the other side of the square."

Juliette shivered. "That doesn't sound very nice."

Emory shrugged with one shoulder. "It's... mostly dry when it rains." He looked away. "And we're given some money for the rats."

Juliette forced herself not to look at the bag. "Is it enough for food?"

"Not really. But we're given food once a day. Stew or bread or perhaps some vegetables." Emory shrugged. "It's good to eat once a day... as long as you bring more than two rats, that is."

"What happens if you don't bring more than two rats?" Juliette asked.

Emory looked away. The smell of the dead rats rose into the air between them.

"I'm sorry," said Juliette, after a long time.

Emory shrugged. "It's not your fault."

They walked to the tenement building in silence. The streets were empty, except for the senseless yammering of a yellow-eyed man on the street, clawing at the air, his cries interspersed with hectic laughter.

Juliette stopped at the door and reached into her pocket. "I... I've been saving you something every day, hoping I might see you." She withdrew a palm-sized bundle wrapped in a bit of newspaper. "It's not much, but maybe it helps."

Emory took it and unwrapped the paper, then stared down at half a stale bread roll, crumbly and squashed from being in Juliette's pocket all day.

"Juli... no." He held it out. "It's yours."

"Not anymore." Juliette pressed his hand back gently. "It's yours now."

Emory stared at the bread, then at her. "Thank you," he whispered.

Juliette bit her lip. "I... I wish you could come and live with us," she blurted out.

Emory's eyes lit up with hope, and Juliette hated herself for crushing it. "I'm sorry. I can't. If I do, if Bert finds out, I know he'll stop paying the rent. I know it." Tears spilled down her cheeks. "I'm sorry, Emory. I can't let Reuben—"

"Hush, hush." Emory put a hand on her arm. "Please, don't cry, Juliette. Don't cry. It's all right. Everything's all right." He smiled somehow. "You don't have to do a thing for me. Just— thank you for the bread. I'll see you again soon."

He let go of her arm and turned to walk away, and Juliette stood in the door for a long time, weeping, so that Reuben wouldn't see her tears.

The truth was that nothing was all right anymore, and maybe it never would be again.

PART III

CHAPTER 11

FIVE YEARS Later

JULIETTE TUGGED at the front of her dress, pulling it tight at the back so that the front would be baggier than ever. It was old and faded and washed almost to oblivion, but Juliette had scraped together a few pennies and bought it anyway to cover the growing curves in her hips and chest. She only knew that those areas were the problem because that was always where boys' eyes went right before they tried to grab her.

She sucked in a deep breath and stepped out of the factory. Dozens of women and children crowded around her, and Juliette tried to lose herself in the group, her heart thudding noisily in her ears. As long as she stayed near the gnarled, half-blind old women and kept her head down, perhaps no one would see her.

But she had only gone halfway down the block when she felt it behind her.

The red-eyed shadow.

"Please," Juliette whispered under her breath. "Please, just go away."

But the shadow never listened. It was on her heels, and she quickened her step, ignoring the curses of the other women as she hastened forward. She spotted her shortcut alleyway and hesitated. Should she go down it? Perhaps the shadow would corner her there.

Then again, up until he'd suddenly vanished a year ago, this was where she used to meet Emory. This was where they exchanged their soft, hesitant kisses.

She plunged down the alleyway, but the manhole cover was closed, and it remained closed even as she stood staring at it. She stumbled up to it and tapped it with her toe. There was nothing.

Her heart felt crushed within her. She had seen Emory less and less over the past eighteen months, until finally, a year ago, he had simply disappeared.

Her knees shook with exhaustion and sorrow, then sprang tight when she heard the voices behind her.

"Think that dress can fool us, do you?" A deep chuckle. "Nothing can obscure that beauty, you pretty thing."

Juliette spun around. She recognized the two men sauntering into the alley, one tall and thin, one short and fat. Both worked in the weaving room of the same cotton mill she worked in. There was a window between the spinning room and the weaving room, and she'd often caught them watching her with the same expression as a stray dog drooling over a rotten bone.

"I'll scream," Juliette panted. "Don't come closer. I'll scream."

"Scream, then," said the first man. "See if anyone cares."

The short one cackled.

Juliette stumbled a step back. The tall one lunged, hands swiping at her, and Juliette turned and bolted.

She ran for all that she was worth, her skirt swishing between her calves, head down, arms pumping. And even though their hideous laughter faded into the distance after a few minutes, Juliette didn't stop running until she had bolted into the tenement building and slammed the door shut behind her.

IT WAS ONLY after several minutes of sitting in the hall, wheezing and coughing, that Juliette caught her breath. She dragged herself to her feet and plodded up the long stairwell, hoping that Reuben had made good on his promise. Otherwise, she would have go out at this hour and look for food for herself and Margie, with strength she simply didn't have.

When she reached the landing, she heard them, and a flood of joy and relief washed through her. Margie was laughing, and a deepening voice joined hers. It was richer and lower than it used to be, but it was still Reuben's laugh, merry and unmistakable.

Juliette pushed the door open. Somehow, Reuben had persuaded Margie to get up and sit at the wooden box that they used as a kitchen table. Her eyes were alight with laughter, and Reuben, now taller than Juliette, stood in front of her, his arms held up over his head.

"You should have heard that poor cat, Marge." He chortled. "The moment Milly spilled that water on its tail, it went 'yoowwwww.' and shot right up the curtain like this." He made clawing motions with his hands.

Margie threw back her head and laughed. Her face was skeletal and pale, but somehow there was still light and love in her eyes, and her laugh was as full and round as if it belonged to a wealthy statesman, not a bony woman skating around the brink of death in this forsaken hole.

"Roo." Juliette closed the door behind her. "You're home."

Reuben spun around. He was tall and lanky now, with long, bony limbs, but there was flesh in his face; his job at a wealthy townhouse was hard, but it fed him three times a day, perhaps for the first time in his life.

"Juli," he cried, wrapping her in a huge hug.

Juliette wondered when he'd gotten so big that she could press her face into his chest. He was still her baby brother, though, and she squeezed him back. "I'm so glad you're here."

"I'm leaving early in the morning, but I'll be home all afternoon tomorrow, right through until Monday morning." Reuben smiled. "I'll bring the rent money then."

"Thank you, poppet," said Margie. "Roo was just telling me all about his day at work, Juli. How was yours?"

Juliette thought of the stifling terror in the alleyway, the two men whose eyes followed her everywhere, and Emory, who failed and failed to come.

"It was fine," she said. "Just fine."

There was a beat of silence. Then Reuben held up a brown paper bag. "I brought bread and cheese. And there's even a bit of ham."

Margie had risen, and now they edged around the wooden box. It was a small one, not quite big enough for three small tin plates, but it still almost filled the tiny tenement. They all three shared a pallet on the nights that Reuben came home. Bert had vanished years ago, and they'd had no choice but to move to an even smaller room.

Still, they took hands and bowed their heads, and Margie's soft voice resounded through the tiny room.

"For what we are about to receive, may the Lord make us truly thankful. Amen."

It was a quiet prayer, but as Juliette tore into her bread, she realized that it was a good one. This moment was imperfect, but she was grateful for it.

She watched the thin white bones moving under Margie's bluish skin and prayed that things would get no worse than this.

IT WAS difficult to imagine how things could get any worse than this.

Emory breathed through his mouth, but somehow, he could still taste the stench that hung in this part of London's sewers. He kept his head down despite the reek that rose from the swampy waters in which he crouched, trembling, waiting for the sound of barking dogs to fade.

The dogs had come upon him a few moments ago. He wasn't sure if they'd been attracted to the squeaking of the rats or the sweet oil that Emory had rubbed on his hands in order to catch the rats. All he knew was that one moment he had seized a rat by its belly, ignoring its bites as he swung it against the wall to kill it, and the next the dogs were bounding through the sewer toward him, barking and snarling. They were only terriers—little more than knee high —but Emory knew from experience that their bites could be deadly. Oh, even the cruellest rat-catcher would seldom allow his dogs to actually tear the throat out of another. But the infection would set in within days, turning a limb green and rotten and dead.

He swallowed a mouthful of air that stank of filth and excrement and kept listening. The barking had stopped. Emory let out a breath of relief and rose slowly to his feet, looking left and right. The sewer's bare brick walls dripped with algae, and piles of rotting rubbish lay everywhere, connected by the streams of dirty water, its surface coated in yellowish scum. There was no sign of the dogs or of their master. Nor any rats, of course. All the racket had scared them away.

Emory sighed. He swung the canvas bag from his shoulder, opened it and gazed at the rat carcasses inside. There were eight. Nowhere near the cosseted target of thirteen a day, but they would feed him, at least, and he knew he needed to get out of his damp clothes quickly if he wanted to avoid catching cold.

Emory swung the bag over his shoulder again and plodded toward the nearest grimy metal ladder, which led to a manhole. He climbed to the top and paused for a minute, listening. It was too early for the factories to have closed, if he guessed right, but he couldn't be too careful.

There were no voices on the other side of the manhole. Emory pushed it open and slipped out, then shoved it back into place with his foot. The familiar alleyway was empty, and Emory felt a swift pang of disappointment.

A part of him had still hoped that Juliette might be here, with her soft eyes and her smooth hair and that smile that made the world seem a little better, if only for a moment. But why would she? It had been a year since he'd last met her in this alley, and it was better that way.

Emory knew he should direct his steps back to the abandoned building where he still lived with the other children that worked for the rat-catcher, but he couldn't stop himself. His feet carried him down the alley and to the left, heading toward the cotton mill.

He scaled a low wall on the corner of the building and landed with a damp squelch of holey socks soaked with sewer water. Quietly, Emory crept around to the small, high window in the back of the factory. He dragged a rubbish bin a little closer and scrambled onto the top, then peered cautiously through the window.

A film of dust and grime covered the glass, but Juliette's brightness shone through it. As always, she was on the spinning floor, watching the giant cotton mule as it clacked and spun. Her pale hair hung down her back, bright as sunshine, and she nibbled her left thumbnail the way she often did when she was worried. Her smooth white brow was furrowed, and her soft eyes were intent on the mule.

Emory let out a long sigh and leaned against the window. She was more beautiful every time he saw her. That happened rarely these days. He knew he should stay away, but he couldn't help trying to see her once every few weeks; blending with the crowd as she walked home, hiding behind a wall as she wandered the market square, even waiting outside her tenement to catch a glimpse of her in the window. Sometimes he saw Reuben, too, looking tall and handsome and healthy. She was breath to his lungs. He didn't know what he would do if he couldn't see her anymore.

Juliette turned, and for a second, their eyes met. Emory's heart leapt into his throat. He wanted to break the window, dive inside and draw her into his arms. He remembered what her soft kisses tasted like, stolen in the alleyway, innocent and gentle and sweet. But as her eyes narrowed, he ducked down and scrambled off the bin, then jogged out of the alley.

He couldn't let Juliette know that he still loved her. It would be better for her if she forgot that he had ever existed. The bag bumped against his hip, making squishy, crunching sounds, and Emory's heart faltered within him.

He had become the scum of this city, a desperate, scrabbling thing that trudged through sewers and killed rodents to stay alive. He had been doing this for too long. He was just like that rat-catcher, reeking and horrible, and shame surrounded him like the stench of human filth.

Worst of all, Juliette would still love him. She would wrap her arms around him no matter how badly he smelled, no matter how infected the cuts and bite marks on his hands, and she deserved better.

No. He had to stay away from Juliette until he could improve himself and become something more.

For now, the glimpse of her would have to be enough. He cradled it in his heart like a precious locket filled with smiles and knew it would keep him warm for days to come.

CHAPTER 12

MARGIE WRITHED ON THE PALLET, a thin arm shoving aside the threadbare blanket. Her hands flexed, the bones of her wrist standing out white against her blue skin.

"No, no," she moaned. "No, please... I still love you."

"Shhhh, Margie." Juliette wiped sweat from her brow. "Shhh. You're all right."

Margie rolled onto her side and let out a terrible cough. It was a dreadful, wet, barking sound, and it chilled Juliette down to her bones.

"Is it the same as Mama had?" Reuben whispered.

Juliette looked across the sleeping pallet at him. He stood in the doorway, clutching a slightly leaky bucket of water from the pump outside. His eyes were very big. She remembered that poor little boy shrieking and crying after their mother had died and wondered how much of it he remembered.

She prayed that he did not remember everything.

"No," she said. "It's not the same thing."

"Are you sure?" Reuben asked.

"Bring me that water," said Juliette.

He shuffled over and handed her the bucket. Juliette plunged a rag into it, wrung it out and rubbed it gently over Margie's forehead, the same movement that she had performed a thousand times for her mother.

"Juli, are you *sure?*" Reuben pressed.

"I—yes." Juliette rubbed the rag over Margie's bony arms. "I'm sure. Mama had whooping cough. She's not whooping." She would never forget the sound of that cough. It was very different to the nasty, wet sound Margie made.

"All right." Reuben bit his lip. "Maybe I should stay here with her. She's not well at all."

Juliette shook her head before he could finish the sentence. "Absolutely not. You're going to work, Roo. They'll dismiss you if you don't."

He sighed but didn't deny it. "Will you stay home with her, then?"

Juliette plunged the rag back into the water. "I'll work something out. Please, Roo, go to work. You're going to be late."

"All right." Reuben grabbed his bag, then crouched down and wrapped an arm around Juliette. "I'll try my best to come home tonight."

"Don't get into trouble," Juliette lectured. "It's not worth it."

"I know, I know." Reuben bent and kissed Margie's forehead. "Feel better soon, Margie."

Margie's eyelids fluttered open. "Roo," she whispered. Then her eyes closed again.

Reuben clumped out of the tenement and disappeared down the stairs, and Juliette listened to the church bell toll five. She needed to leave very soon if she was going to get to the factory on time.

"But what about you, Margie?" she whispered. "How can I leave you all alone?"

Margie rolled onto her side, her bony body shuddering with another fit of coughs. Juliette pulled the blankets over her again and tucked her in. "You won't stay warm if I'm not here," she whispered.

Margie shivered with fever. Juliette didn't know whether to warm her or cool her down. She needed medicine, more than anything, but there was no money for that. There never had been.

Maybe, if she stayed away today, she could tell the overseer she'd been sick. Perhaps then he would forgive her. But she remembered the girl who had been home with brown lung for a single day last year. When she returned, the overseer beat her and threw her onto the streets, sobbing and covered in angry red welts.

Juliette shuddered. She couldn't lose her job at the factory; without it, they would have nowhere to live and nothing to eat. And what would become of Margie then?

"Juli?" Margie whispered. Her eyes were open, and there was a flicker of lucidity in them.

"It's all right, Margie," said Juliette. She smoothed the blankets over Margie's shoulders. "You'll be all right."

Margie's fever-reddened eyes found Juliette's. "You'll..." She sucked in a rattling breath. "You'll be late for work."

"Don't worry about that now," Juliette soothed. "I can't leave you all on your own." Even as she said it, she knew that she had to.

Margie shook her head feebly, her damp, dirty hair stirring on her pillow. "No. No... you have to go."

Juliette swallowed hard, fighting the tears that burned the corners of her eyes. "Margie..."

"I'll be fine," Margie whispered. "Don't lose your job on account of me, poppet."

Juliette brushed a strand of dirty hair from Margie's face. "But what about you?"

"I'll be just fine," said Margie.

"I'm sorry," said Juliette.

Margie's bony hand found Juliette's and squeezed it. "Don't be. You... you're a miracle, do you know that?"

"I'll be back as soon as I can," said Juliette.

Margie nodded, and her hand slackened on Juliette's.

The bell tolled a quarter past five. She had to go. Juliette rearranged the blankets as well as she could and tiptoed to the door, but Margie had not fallen asleep. Her weak croak reached Juliette as she laid a hand on the door.

"Juli?"

Juliette turned back. "Yes, Margie?"

Margie was lying very still, but her eyes were bright. "You know that I love you, don't you?" she said. "That I've loved you and Roo from the moment I first laid eyes on you?"

Juliette swallowed the fat lump in her throat. "I do."

Margie's eyes fluttered closed. Juliette closed the door.

JULIETTE STEPPED out of the tenement building and into a bitter, sleeting morning. The sun was still far from rising. Street lamps cast pools of pale-yellow light, watery as urine, onto the frosted cobblestones. Juliette pulled her thin collar up to her chin and hunkered her head down between her shoulders. The crowd had already thinned as workers made their way to the factories. She had no time to waste.

Still, striding down that street made Juliette feel as though she dragged her head behind her like a ball and chain. It wanted to stay up in that tenement with Margie and make sure that she would be all right.

You didn't make sure that Mama was all right, a taunting voice told her in the back of her mind. Ever since Reuben had started working at the townhouse and Emory had vanished, that voice was growing more and more difficult to ignore. Juliette wiped sleet from her face and walked faster.

She had not yet reached the end of the block when she felt the pressure of eyes upon her and whirled around. Her heart leapt into her mouth. For an instant, she thought she saw his silhouette in the plodding crowd, tall and lanky, smile cocked at a jaunty angle.

But there was nothing. Just the sleet driving against her face, and a scowling, stinking man who bumped into her and stormed off without an apology.

Juliette's belly tightened. If it wasn't Emory whose eyes she felt upon her...

She shrank back a few steps. It had to be the red-eyed shadow, because the more she searched, the more certain she felt that something was watching her.

"Don't be a fool, Juli," she whispered to herself. "It's just a childhood fear. It's not real." But the terror that thudded in her blood was as real as the breath in her lungs.

Something stirred in the shadows of the building. Juliette's head snapped around to stare at it, but it was gone, and the building's door was just swinging shut. She was imagining it, she told herself. Someone had simply walked into the building. There was nothing sinister about that.

Her eyes darted up to the window of the third floor, and her heart stammered in her chest. The shadow was after Margie—

"Juliette, *no*." She turned around and jogged in the direction of work. There was no time for this foolish old fear of hers.

Still, it dogged her all the way to work, and pursued her through every moment of another long, exhausting day.

❦

EMORY'S FINGERS FLEXED, open and closed, as he stared through the window of the scruffy little pawnshop.

It was quiet that day. When Saturday came, Emory knew that the shop would be full of patrons, come to pawn their goods in order to afford Monday morning's rent. Now, though, there was only one fat man poring over the rows of cheap items in the glass case under the counter. The clerk behind the counter gazed at nothing, bored.

It wasn't the clerk that caught Emory's eye, however. It was the sign glued to the window, handwritten in messy letters. Emory couldn't read, but one of the other rat-catcher children had taught him the shape of one key word: VACANCY.

It meant a job. And a job could mean everything to Emory... especially getting to see Juliette again.

He squared his shoulders, took a deep breath, and pushed open the door. The clerk raised his head and narrowed his eyes, looking up and down Emory's scruffy frame. He had tried his best, after dropping off his day's quota of rats at the abandoned building, to wash his grimy and bloodstained hands under the pump despite the bitter cold. He had even tried to dunk his head under the stream of frigid water, but a bobby had spotted him and driven him away.

Emory gave the clerk his most winning smile and opened his mouth, but the other man beat him to it.

"We don't buy stolen goods," he grunted. "Go and find another fence for your rubbish."

"Oh, no, sir," said Emory. "I'm not here to—"

"I don't want to hear it." The clerk waved a hand. "Get out."

The fat man stared at them both. Emory hesitated. "Sir, I'm just looking for—"

"We don't serve the likes of you here," the clerk sneered.

Emory summoned his courage. "Sir, I want to apply to your—"

The clerk reached under the counter and withdrew a black-jack. "Get out."

The fat man stared at Emory in disgust, his lip curling, and Emory knew how this would end if he persisted; with a beating, with the shriek of police whistles, with nothing but trouble. He hung his head and ducked out of the shop, then jogged down the street until he couldn't hear the clerk's angry cries anymore.

Sleet pattered on his hat and the back of his coat, soaking slowly to his skin. Emory sighed deeply. He had no choice but to go back to the abandoned building where he lived now.

He thrust his hands deep into the pockets of his coat, avoiding the holes in the bottom, and turned his aching feet for home. A missed opportunity like this always felt like a punch to the belly. It was rare that Emory caught thirteen rats in a single day, and when he did, he always did the same thing: turned them in, took his few pennies, and then hurried out to the street for a piece of bread and something far more important—a precious few hours' search for a new job.

If he could only become a slopworker, a sweeper, a factory worker—anything that would allow him to pay a little rent and have somewhere to wash away the stench of the sewer— then perhaps he would be able to look Juliette in the eye again. Yet the more he tried, the more he was chased away.

He stopped in front of a grimy windowpane in the market square where he had had the best moments of his life with Juliette and Reuben. There was no chance of running into Juliette now; it was late afternoon on a workday, and she would be in the factory. He ignored the delicious smells of baking bread and bubbling stew rising from the square and stared at his reflection in the dirty glass. The rat-catcher insisted on shaving the hair of all the children once every six months to stop lice, and he had done so just a few days ago. Under Emory's cap, only a faint dusting of hair had reappeared. His face was pale and pasty from spending most of his days in the sewers, and there were several half-healed bites and scratches on his cheeks, accompanied by smears of dirt where his attempt at washing had failed.

He wore shoes with soles that had begun to disintegrate, offering a glimpse of the pale flesh of his toes. His coat hung in tatters from his frame, stained beyond recognition, threads trailing from the frayed hem. Even his trousers were hopelessly frayed, often patched, the patches themselves coming to pieces.

A deep sigh shook the length of Emory's frame, and he turned away, tears prickling behind his eyes. He looked appalling.

Not like a human being anymore, but a phantasm of filth and horror. It was no wonder nobody would listen when he asked for work; no one saw him as a person.

If he could only lay his hands on better clothes, perhaps his luck would change. But in order to get better clothes, he needed money. He was trapped in an endless circle of hopeless need.

He lowered his head against the sleet that stung the back of his neck and trudged away from the square and into the narrow, twisting streets that led to the warehouse. His eyes were so trained on his feet that he didn't see the man until he was almost upon him.

Emory stumbled to a halt, his heart jumping to his throat. This street was narrow and dark, with windowless walls on either side, and he'd come across many a jabbering victim of opium here. But this was different. This man wasn't jabbering or twitching or sniffing or doing anything at all. He lay flat on his face, arms spread out by his sides. A torn paper bag lay beside him, dark glass glinting dully in the fading light, and clean clothes spilled out of a leather satchel by his side.

"Sir?" Emory called, his voice thready and nervous.

The man didn't stir. Emory glanced around, but there was no one to be seen. The man's clothes were sturdy and warm; he wasn't from around here. If Emory just left him here, the scoundrels of this part of town would strip him naked and leave him to freeze.

"Sir," Emory called. He shuffled over to the man and prodded his hip with his toe. "Sir, you can't sleep here."

The man didn't move. Emory's heart squeezed in his chest. He stepped back, suddenly wanting nothing to do with him, but what if he was still alive and needed help?

Though it made his hands burn with fear, Emory crouched down, grasped the man's arm, and flipped him over onto his back. He rolled up to face the sky, and his face was pasty pale, streaked with ugly blotches of deep purple. The swollen tongue protruded between his teeth, and his eyes were glassy and empty of any life.

Emory screamed and sprang back. The man's body reeked of old ale, and a puncture mark in his arm told the story of how he had come to be like this.

Death. Emory was surrounded by so much death. He slept in a warehouse filled with dead rats, many of which he'd killed. He stumbled upon so many bodies down in the sewers, washed up by the Thames. Nausea roiled in his belly, and Emory turned to flee, but as he did so, a flash of white caught his eye.

He froze and stared at the satchel. *Clothes.*

They were decent, too, at least as decent as the ones the man was wearing. He glimpsed a sturdy white cotton shirt, a proper one with a collar and real buttons, and all the buttons matched. There were trousers, too. He didn't see a single patch on them.

Emory knew he should walk away, but he couldn't stop himself from shuffling closer and picking up the satchel. The shirt was too white to touch with his filthy hands, but he pulled the pants out and held them against himself.

They would be a perfect fit, which was strange, for the dead man was significantly bigger than he was.

Emory's heart thudded in his ears. If he could don these and smooth down his hair and walk back into that pawnshop, he knew that the clerk wouldn't even recognize him. Much less would anyone judge him who had never seen him before. They could give him a chance, a real chance, at a better job.

No. Emory closed the satchel and extended an arm, ready to drop it. The dead man might have no use for these things, but it still felt wrong to take them. But his fingers wouldn't open.

If he had a better job, if he dressed better, then perhaps he would be worthy of Juliette.

The memory of her smile flooded his soul, lighting him up from within. The thought of having a single conversation with her... It took his breath away. As he stared at the satchel, he dared to wonder if there could be more to seeing her again. If he could find a job that was so much better that he could improve *her* life.

"Oh, Juliette," he whispered, a hot tear rolling down his cheek.

She was alive. The man at his feet was not.

Emory slung the satchel over his shoulder and fled at a dead run.

CHAPTER 13

DESPITE THE PERSISTENT, throbbing ache in Juliette's thighs, she plunged up the stairs two at a time, her feet clattering heavily on the wood. The bag over her shoulder was as empty as her stomach, yet she didn't care now. She just needed to get back to the tenement.

Her lungs ached from running as much of the way home as she possibly could, and her dress was splashed with slush. It pressed coldly against her knees as she hiked them up high and bolted the last few steps onto the landing.

"Margie," she called out, rushing to the door. "Margie, I'm here."

There was no response. In the few seconds that it took Juliette to run down the hall to the door, the vivid image of her mother's dead body flashed through her mind. Only this time the pale blue, blotchy face was not her mother's. It was Margie's.

What would she tell Reuben?

"Margie," Juliette cried and shoved the door open.

Her eyes flew to the sleeping pallet, and a pang of relief assailed her. Margie wasn't there. Her weak knees nearly gave out with sheer relief, and she clutched the doorframe to stay upright.

"Oh, Margie, I was so worried," Juliette gushed. "What—"

She stopped. There was no one by the stove, either. No one by the crate they used as a table.

It didn't take but a second to look across the whole tenement; it was a single room, only a few square feet, but Margie wasn't there.

Juliette clasped her hands to her mouth, her breaths coming in terrified, ragged gasps. She stumbled into the room and turned in a circle, as though she could have missed Margie somewhere behind the tiny box or the low pallet, but there was no sign of her.

"Margie?" she croaked. Her mouth was utterly dry. "Margie?"

No one responded. Juliette's heart felt as though it had swollen so big that it crushed the breath from her lungs. She stumbled into the hallway and screamed, "Margie!"

Her thoughts flew wildly to the time when Margie was less sick, a few years ago, when the hallways of this rotten building were always swept clean, and the stairs always scrubbed. But cobwebs hung like blankets in the corners now, and the walls were thick with dust. Margie hadn't been strong enough to clean for a long time. Yet where else could she be? She could see the toilet door down the hall hanging open. It was empty.

Juliette ran down the stairs to the second floor. "Margie. *Margie!*"

The first floor was the same, the ground floor too. Margie wasn't anywhere to be seen. Juliette ran onto the street, empty and dark now, and cupped her hands around her mouth to scream her friend's name. There was no response except screams and cackles from the homeless men across the street.

Her heart racing, Juliette ran back up the stairs. She flung herself against the first door on the third floor and hammered on the wood with the same terrible despair she had felt on the night Beatrice died. There was no response, and she staggered to the next door; this one looked too flimsy for knocking, so she slammed her fist against the wall instead.

"Hello? Hello. Hello," she screamed.

The door swung open, and a huge, reeking man towered over her, a cigarette drooping damply from his lower lip. "What?" he hissed, spraying her with saliva.

Juliette summoned her courage. Nothing, nothing could be worse than going back to that empty tenement. "Margie. The lady who lives in number thirty-seven. Where is she?"

"Don't know," the man grunted, and slammed the door, almost crushing Juliette's fingers.

She turned and stumbled to the next door, but there was only an angry old lady behind this one, who spat and cursed at her. Babies began to cry, and curses and screams resounded through the building as Juliette stumbled from one door to the next, begging for help. No one cared to help her. Few even knew who Margie was.

Juliette was sobbing and numb with terror when she reached the last door on the third floor. Her body trembled uncontrollably as she raised a fist to knock. Before her knuckles could touch the wood, the door swung open, and a thin woman with a baby on her hip gave her a tired stare out of red eyes. The baby was crying feebly.

Juliette cowered, ready for a blow, but the woman simply said, "Yes?"

Was it possible that someone with a kind heart still existed in this building? "I—I'm looking for my friend." Juliette rubbed her knuckles over her tear-streaked cheeks. "Her name is Margie. She—"

"Oh, I know her, I think." The woman, incredibly, mustered a smile. "Didn't she always used to sweep the floors and dust the corners, a few years ago?"

Juliette nodded fast. "Yes, yes, yes, that's her. She was here when I left this morning, but now she's gone. Please." She swallowed hard. "I have to find her."

"I thought she'd died, you know, but then I saw her this afternoon," said the woman.

Juliette gasped. "You saw her?"

"Yes. She looked very ill, poor lady. It's so sad, isn't it? She was always such a dear." The woman bounced her baby, who kept crying.

"Was she—" Juliette gulped. "Alive?"

"Oh, yes, she was. She even looked happy," said the woman. "She was with a man."

Juliette braced a hand against the wall to keep from falling. "A man? Who?"

"I don't know, dear. I'm not very good with faces. I only remember Margie because of how lovely she always was."

"What did he look like?" Juliette rasped. "Did he have a big nose... was he angry?"

Of course, Margie would be happy if Bert came to fetch her. There was a part of her that would always love him, that would always believe in him.

But the woman was slowly shaking her head. "No... no. Are you thinking of her husband?"

"Yes," Juliette gasped.

"I remember him. Always came stamping in here, waking the children." The woman cradled her baby protectively. "It definitely wasn't him. No, this was a handsome man, some years older, you know? He had strong arms and legs, and a nice smile. Freckles, too. I liked him."

Juliette leaned her head against the wall, biting back a sob. She didn't know anyone who matched the woman's description.

"Are you all right, dear?" the woman asked.

"Did you see where they went?" Juliette whispered.

The woman shook her head. "I'm so sorry, dear. I didn't."

"Thank you." Juliette dragged the back of her hand across her eyes. "Thank you very much." She hesitated. "You said... you said she looked happy?"

"It was hard to tell, dear, because she was so weak, she could barely walk. She was soaked through with sweat, poor mite. Her face was so pale. I think she hardly knew what was happening," said the woman. "But I know she was smiling."

"Mama," a small voice screamed from inside the tenement.

"I'm sorry, dear. I hope you find her," said the woman, and shut the door.

Juliette sagged to the ground. Grief crushed her like a great stone between her shoulders, and she pressed her forearms against the floor, a keening sob escaping her lips. She lowered her head until her forehead pressed against her fingers and sucked in a shaking breath, then sobbed again.

"Juliette?"

The scared voice was Reuben's. Juliette flew to her feet, tamping down her grief as quickly as she could, but it was too late. Reuben was already scared to death. His face was ashen as he ran to Juliette and grabbed her hands. "Juli, what's wrong? Are you hurt? Are you sick? Is it—"

"I'm fine," said Juliette. "I'm fine."

"But what's wrong?" he begged. "Look at you. You're so pale." He stopped, and terror filled his eyes. "Margie?"

"Roo—" Juliette began.

He tore away from her and ran across the hallway to their tenement.

"Roo, wait," Juliette called. "It's not what you think."

Reuben ripped the door open with such force that he nearly tore it from its hinges. He crashed into the room and let out a shriek. "*No*. No."

Juliette stumbled into the tenement after him. "Reuben—"

He whirled around. "You already had her taken away?" he cried. "I didn't have the chance to say goodbye."

"She's not dead, Reuben." Juliette hollered.

Reuben stopped. His face crumpled with sorrow, and his hands were shaking. "I don't understand. What happened? Where is she?"

"I don't know." Juliette couldn't hold back her own sobs. "Someone took her away."

His face darkened. "Bert."

"No. Someone saw her leave... she said it wasn't with Bert. It was with another man. I don't know who it could be." Juliette covered her mouth with her hands. "But I don't know where he took her."

Reuben sagged onto the sleeping pallet, tears rolling down his cheeks. "She wouldn't leave us, Juli. Why would she leave us?"

"I don't know." Juliette wished she had something better to offer.

Reuben stared at her, the tears coming faster. "We have to find her."

"But how?" Juliette asked.

He shook his head. "We just have to. Come on."

Reuben rose to his feet, grabbed Juliette's hand and dragged her into the street. And though they called and called until the bell tolled four and they had to go to work, there was no sign of Margie, nor of her mysterious kidnapper.

JULIETTE STOOD motionless in the bustling street. It had been more than a day since she had slept, and it felt as though her feet couldn't possibly carry her another step, but that wasn't why she stood so very still. Workers pushed past her, shoving her a foot this way, a foot that way, but she barely felt them through her haze of grief and exhaustion.

She blinked, her eyes filling like they'd been filled with sand. Something was missing.

Juliette frowned and looked around. It felt as though something had been ripped from her world, like the time when a factory on this street had burned down and the gap between buildings had felt like a lost tooth for weeks. This was a subtler loss than the ripping emptiness of knowing that Margie wouldn't be home when she returned tonight. No, this sense of something missing was quiet and strangely peaceful.

Juliette took a staggering step forward, then another, and another. It was only when she reached the tenement building that she realized what it was that she hadn't felt once on the way home, for the first time in her life.

Her belly knotted as she looked around.

There was no red-eyed shadow today. Nothing was following her home.

She stared at the building, shaking. Maybe it was just a child-hood fear, after all, and maybe losing Margie had shown her that there were far worse things than some sinister, imaginary phantom.

But she was inclined to believe the suspicion deep inside her soul: that whatever or whoever the red-eyed shadow was, it had taken Margie away from her.

PART IV

CHAPTER 14

ONE YEAR Later

IT WAS the silence that was the worst part.

Juliette's new tenement was still in the same building, but it was on the ground floor, the coldest and dampest of them all. It had no windows, and if she stood up and stretched out her arms, she could brush her fingertips against the opposite walls. There was a door, true, but it was made from a bit of smelly, salty driftwood, suspended on hinges made of string.

She sat facing the door now, her back against the wall. It was damp and smelled of mould, but she was just too tired to sit upright. Her breath rattled in her chest as she spooned up another mouthful of cold gruel she'd cooked the night before.

It hadn't been enough even for one meal, and she had divided it into two. The gruel was grey and stodgy and flavourless, but she savoured every bite, convincing herself that it was enough somehow.

But the gruel, the damp, the cold, the size of the room—none of these hard things were the hardest. It was the silence that was suffocating her.

Of course, the building was never completely silent. She could always feel the pressure of dozens of aching souls all around her. People snored and coughed, argued in raised voices, and yammered gibberish late into the night. Babies screamed; occasionally, incredibly, a child would laugh, a brief thread of brightness through this dark tapestry of human desperation. Yet all that sound only accentuated the quiet here within the four tilting walls of Juliette's tiny room. The chatter made her lack of company all the more deafening.

She finished her gruel and wiped out the tiny tin bowl with a rag and some cold water, then lay down on the narrow pallet that barely fit inside this room. When she rolled the blanket around herself, it was nearly warm. Eyes closed, Juliette lay waiting for sleep to take her, praying quietly for Reuben. He was a footman now, and she was so proud of him. Beatrice would have loved to see him in his livery.

Her thoughts wandered as sleep stole across her mind. Margie, too, would be so impressed to see Reuben now. Juliette had cut a picture of him out of the paper; distant and blurred, of course, as the picture had been taken of the prestigious family he worked for, and Reuben had simply happened to be standing by the carriage door. She reached inside her dress and touched the curled, faded edge of the paper, although it was too dark to look at it now. She wished she could show it to Margie.

But she was long gone. Juliette and Reuben had abandoned their search of her six months ago, when Reuben had been promoted and let Juliette know that he would only be able to come home to her on Sunday afternoons for a few hours.

She had slept every night in this tiny new tenement alone.

A single tear escaped down her cheek as she clutched the piece of newspaper in her hand, but sobbing would only make her sore, rattling lungs ache. So she breathed deeply, slowly, and tried to think of nothing at all until she finally slept.

JULIETTE'S NECK and shoulders ached fiercely. She rolled her head left and right, trying to ease some of the agonizing tension, but the movement sent a pang through her inflamed throat. She groaned and bowed her head, but it was too late to stop the coughs. They ripped through her chest, bending her double, and she covered her face with one arm and spluttered hopelessly into her sleeve.

By the time the fit had passed, she was gasping for breath. The workers around her, as shabby and dusty as she was, gave her a wide berth. Several glanced at her sideways, as though they expected her to drop dead at any moment.

Juliette couldn't blame them. She'd seen the very same thing happen to people with brown lung.

She dragged her sleeve over her nose to wipe it and plodded onward, nearly home. Brown lung? She pushed the thought away. No... she couldn't have it. But how many years had it been at that factory? How much longer could she last?

She had to be strong for Reuben, she told herself. But did she? He was all right without her. Her mother was gone. Margie and Emory were gone. Reuben was happy and safe.

Juliette could get sick now, she thought, and no one would care except for Reuben. And he would be sad, but he wouldn't starve.

The thought frightened her, made the earth feel about to crack under her feet, so she tucked her head down and walked faster. It reminded her of her old fear of the red-eyed shadow, but it had been months since the last time she looked over her shoulder. The shadow had gotten what it wanted: it had taken Margie. Ever since, it had left her alone.

"Stop that," Juliette told herself under her breath. "You're *not* going to feel sorry for yourself, Juli. You're going to get through this."

She prayed silently for strength, but still felt little. Just enough to drag herself up to the door of the tenement. A faint throb of despairing nervousness ran through her when she saw the stooped gentleman by the front door. He couldn't be a tenant here, Juliette was sure; he was dressed too nicely for that, although not by much. Perhaps he was a client of that scruffy girl in number sixteen.

She kept her head down and went to push past him, and that was when he spoke.

"Juliette?"

The voice was like a great shaft of brilliant sunshine spilling over her head after two years of winter. Juliette let out a scream and whirled around. A cough wrenched from her lungs, and for an instant she was certain that she was delirious or dying.

But then he stepped forward into the faint light from the feeble gas lamp over the door, and she knew that he was real. Taller, his face filled with colour, his shoulders filled out, but there was no mistaking the smile that tilted at an angle as cheerful as that of his sturdy tweed cap.

Juliette clasped her hands over her chest. "Emory?" she cried. "Can it be?"

He stepped forward and held out his hands. "It is."

Juliette couldn't move. She could only stare at him, drinking in every detail: the smooth sweep of his clean, glossy hair over his forehead, the strong lines of his chest against the patched yet warm coat he was wearing, the shoes that were old and battered yet bore evidence of a little polish, the warmth of his soft eyes, the glory of that familiar smile.

"I know it must be strange to see me again after all these years," said Emory softly. "If you wish me to go, I'll go." He spoke better, too. "But I couldn't stay away. I had to see you to see if you still—" He stuttered. "If you still feel about me as I feel about you. If you don't—"

Juliette didn't let him finish. She rushed forward, her veins filled with new strength, and seized his hands in both of hers. He let out a faint yelp of surprise as she pulled him close and pressed her lips to his, her heart singing in her chest. It was a brief kiss, yet tender, and when he returned it, Juliette's heart spun in mad cartwheels.

He drew back, his eyes shining in the faint light. "Juli."

"Emory," Juliette sobbed, and fell into his warm embrace.

They held each other for longer than was really proper, and when they began to draw disapproving glances from the handful of stragglers still moving through the streets, Juliette stepped back. She didn't know if she was laughing or crying; all she knew was that her prayer had been answered.

"Where have you been?" she asked. "All this time…"

Emory looked away. "I was here," he said quietly. "Catching rats for that horrid man. But I wasn't the person you see now, Juli. I was—" He choked.

"Did something happen?" Juliette asked.

"I was ashamed." Emory met her eyes. "I was barely human. Scrabbling in those sewers, grabbing those rodents with my bare hands—" He shuddered. "It was terrible. I smelled terrible, felt terrible. I couldn't face you like that."

The shame in his eyes broke Juliette's heart.

"So I watched you... when I could." Emory swallowed. "I tried to make sure you were all right, but there was nothing I could do for you."

"Oh, Emory." Juliette reached up and cupped his face in her hands. If she had felt any flicker of anger, it vanished at the love and joy and relief in his eyes. "You never had to *do* anything for me. Who you *are* has always been enough."

Emory's eyes closed for a moment, and warm tears coursed down his cheeks. He placed his big, warm hands over hers. "I've missed you so much."

"I've missed you too," said Juliette. She hesitated. "Do you... do you know where Margie is?"

He frowned. "What do you mean, where Margie is?"

"Someone took her. Not Bert—I don't know who. But someone." Juliette bit her lip.

"I'm sorry. I don't know." Emory wrapped his hands around hers. "But I'll help you find her. I can help you again now, Juli." He grinned. "I've found work, good, honest work at a pottery factory. I make tiles. I've been there about six months now, after a gift from God that came at my lowest point."

"A gift from God?" Juliette asked.

"I thought it was a failure on my part at first, but you know He has a way of turning things around. I'll tell you all about it sometime." Emory beamed. "It's not a wonderful job, but it's good enough that I've been able to get a little tenement of my own, a bit better than this one. And I think things might improve for me. The supervisor is kind in his way, and I've worked hard to prove myself to him."

"Oh, Emory, this is wonderful." Juliette squeezed his hands.

"I'm trying to learn to read, too. It's not easy, but one of the men in my building helps me at times," said Emory.

"I can help, too. Well—we can help each other. I learned a few bits from Margie. It's been a long time, but I can try to remember," said Juliette. "Now that I can see you again."

"Yes... yes." Emory paused. "I won't be able to see you often, Juli. We both know how long the hours are at factories. But it's only for now. Until my job improves. Then..." He paused, and the glorious promise in his eyes made Juliette's heart turn cartwheels.

They stayed up far too late that night, sitting on the steps and talking. The cold was bitter, but Juliette didn't care. What could possibly matter compared to sitting here with Emory for the first time in years?

Finally, when the bell tolled just once, Emory got to his feet. "I'll see you on Sunday, Juli." He smiled, his eyes twinkling. "And in the meantime, I'll think of ways we can look for Margie."

"Thank you," said Juliette. "Thank you so much."

Emory raised his eyebrows. "What for? I haven't done anything yet."

She took his hand and squeezed it tightly. "You've given me hope."

And she'd had none of that for a long, long time.

CHAPTER 15

IT FELT as though Juliette had seen no sunshine in the two long years of Emory's disappearance. Now, though, as spring gave way at last to summer, it felt as though regular patches of it drifted through her life. She felt better, too, as if Emory's very presence had somehow healed her.

She hadn't even known that there was a park just a few blocks away from the gloomy tenement building where she had lived out her entire life. She couldn't remember if she had ever felt green grass beneath her feet—beneath her threadbare shoes, at least—until the first time Emory had brought her here about two months ago, shortly after his sudden return.

Now, balmy sunlight poured down on the park. The London bushes that lined its edges were filled with green leaves that rustled throatily in the breeze. The grass was long and unkempt, and there were weeds growing along the tumble-down wooden fence instead of flowers, but to Juliette it felt like another world.

"This is wonderful, Emory." She lowered the bowl of rich, warm rabbit stew he'd bought for her.

Emory beamed. "It's good to be able to give you a full belly." He rested a hand very cautiously, very lightly on her arm. "Hopefully, someday soon, I can give you much more."

Juliette leaned against the bench and allowed herself to dream just a little, of a cottage, maybe with a strip of lawn, and children laughing. But only if there was money for food and medicine. She didn't want any child to lose as much as she had lost.

There was laughter from the grimy pond at one end of the park, and Reuben tossed a tiny bit of bread crust to the ducks. Not long ago, he would have wolfed it down and considered it a full meal. Now, in part thanks to the occasional treat that Emory was able to give them, his limbs were growing broad and strong.

"I'm just sorry we haven't found Margie yet," Emory murmured.

Juliette laid a hand over his. "Someday," she said. She prayed for it every night.

She prayed for more too, now that she had the hope to do so. She prayed that things would change. A month ago, walking in the park and smiling into Emory's eyes had been enough, but now she wondered if they would ever progress. If she would ever escape that tumbledown tenement.

Emory squeezed his hand as though reading her mind. "Someday," he promised. "Someday."

❦

Someday came just a few weeks later on a cloudy evening, with the promise of a storm hovering yellow and grubby over the city, and it came out of nowhere.

The factory closed a little earlier on Saturday nights. Juliette was grateful for it; it meant that she could make it home in time to sleep for the one full night a week that she had. Tomorrow, she might see Emory, if he could get away from work for a few hours. She could be excited if she tried hard enough, but right at that moment, she had no strength left for trying.

Her shoes shuffled loudly as she walked, the loose soles snapping, and Juliette tried her best to take slow, deep breaths. Each one sent a fresh burst of pain through her lungs. She held back a cough, knowing it would only produce a glob of dirty sputum, and wondered what she would tell Emory when he asked her how she felt tomorrow.

"Fine," she'd say, even though she knew that the illness had come back, and she was getting worse. Just a few months ago, she'd been able to breathe freely on Saturdays, when her body had adjusted to the foulness of the cotton mill. Now, if Saturday felt like this, Monday would be unbearable.

She squared her shoulders, trying to shake off the gloom as she took the last turn back to her tenement building. Emory had promised her that things would change someday. She had to hold firmly to that promise; it was all that she had.

A cold thrill ran down the length of her spine out of the blue. Juliette stumbled to a halt. Her head snapped left and right, and her breaths came faster, hairs rising on the back of her neck. When she whirled around, there was nothing on the street behind her except for the handful of workers still struggling home.

It couldn't be... surely it couldn't be. That had simply been a silly old childhood fear.

Juliette's heart thudded against her ribs. She took deep breaths, but her feet wouldn't move. Even though her mind told her that it was impossible, every fibre of her body screamed the same thing: the red-eyed shadow was back, and it was watching her.

It felt as though her feet had melded with the cobblestones. Juliette had never felt that intense presence nearer than at that moment, and even as her rational mind struggled against the thought, she knew it was coming closer, and she knew with a deep and primal part of herself that it wanted her.

A male voice spoke directly behind her. "Juliette? Juliette Purcell?"

Juliette screamed and whipped around. The shadow was upon her. He was tall and broad-shouldered, his head grotesquely deformed as his silhouette loomed over her outside the light of the nearest streetlamp.

Fear flooded Juliette's blood like ice. She spun around, and the shadow snatched her arm, clutching it in an iron grip.

"Juliette," the shadow barked.

Juliette wanted to scream, but she was consumed with trying to wrench herself free from that grip. The shadow had captured her. It was going to destroy her—

"Juliette, stop!" the shadow cried. "Margie sent me."

Juliette froze. She hadn't heard anyone other than herself, Reuben or Emory—the three little rabbits—say that name in more than a year.

"What?" she gasped.

Her captor stepped into the light, and he was no shadow, but a sturdy man in sun-faded clothes. His eyes were brown, not red, and he had a broad, pleasant, freckled face, ruddy and wrinkled. It held a kindness that Juliette had seldom seen here in London, except in Margie's eyes. When he spoke, his accent was slow and rounded, like Margie's but deeper and thicker. And the tuft of hair that sprouted from beneath his tweed cap was the same mousy colour as Margie's.

"I'm sorry. I didn't mean to scare you," he said, releasing her arm. "Please don't fret. I'm not going to hurt you."

Juliette backed away a few steps, rubbing her arm where he had grabbed her. There was no pain, but she still felt the echo of his grip, and the wild hope in her heart was easily drowned out by her terror.

"What do you want?" she cried. "Who are you?"

The man spread his hands. "My name is Ralph. I'm Margie's brother."

Juliette's jaw dropped. "You're... you're *her* Ralph?"

"I am," he said. "I know it's difficult for you to believe me, but I am."

Juliette pressed her fingertips to her bottom lip. "Where is she?" she whispered. "Is she... still alive?"

Ralph's smile was warm and kind. "Yes. She's alive and, after a long, long illness, she is well, too. And she's asking for you and Reuben."

Dared she believe it? Juliette wasn't sure, but her heart was hammering wildly in her chest. "How can I be sure you're telling the truth?"

"Margie was right." Ralph sighed. "She warned me that this city twists people into something that they never used to be. She told me not to be put off if you were scared or suspicious. You've had to be, to survive here."

Juliette took another step back.

"Don't go. Please. I can prove it to you." Ralph held up a hand. "Margie told me all about you and your brother. Your mother's name was Beatrice, and you lost her to whooping cough six, nearly seven years ago now. You were just a little girl. You used to spend time with Margie when she was cleaning the hallways of your building. She liked to try teaching you to read; you were brilliant, she said."

Tears stung Juliette's eyes as the memories came flooding back.

"It took Margie a long time to convince Bert to let you and Reuben stay with them, but she did. And even after Bert was long gone, you and Reuben stayed true to her right up until the moment that I came to get her," said Ralph.

"You came to get her?" Juliette cried. He certainly matched the description the young woman had given her.

"Yes." Ralph looked away. "I should have done it earlier. Much earlier... But that's a long story." He paused. "The short and long of it is, Juliette, that Margie was ill, very ill, for more than a year. It's only recently that she has been up and about and able to care for herself a little again. And the first thing she asked me, when her wits were about her, was if I knew what had become of you and Reuben. I promised her I would come and find you both. She wants to see you, but she's not well enough to travel. I want to take you to her."

"Oh." Juliette gasped. She covered her face with her hands, overcome, and hot tears oozed between her fingers.

"I know this must be a great shock to you," said Ralph.

Juliette lowered her hands. Could it be? It had to be. No one would know everything that Ralph had just told them, unless they'd spoken to Margie, and the resemblance was powerful.

"You can really take us to Margie?" she whispered. "In the country... on the farm she told us about?"

"I can," said Ralph, "and I shall, if you'll let me. In fact, I have a carriage waiting. We can go at once."

"At once." Juliette clapped her hands over her mouth. "But Reuben's not here."

"Where is he?" Ralph asked.

"At work. He's a footman now. He sometimes comes to see me on a Sunday, but I don't even know where the house is," Juliette admitted.

Ralph rubbed the back of his neck. "Well, we can't leave him. It's very late now. I will find lodging for tonight, and then come for you again in the morning. As soon as Reuben comes to your home, we can leave for the country."

Juliette thought of Reuben's face when she told him the good news, and a laugh tore free. She hadn't laughed this freely, except with Emory, since she could remember. "Yes, yes. Thank you, Ralph. Thank you so much for all of the good news."

"No, Juliette." Ralph reached out cautiously and folded his big hands around hers. They were rough and work-worn, but their touch was gentle. "Thank *you*. If it hadn't been for the love you and your brother lavished on Margie—" His eyes filled with tears. "I owe you both the world."

He strode away, leaving Juliette to her tenement. She lay awake for a long time that night, trying to be sure that none of this had been a happy dream.

But it was not. The next morning, when Reuben arrived home from work, Ralph and Juliette were waiting for him at the door. And when Juliette told him everything, he cried with joy until he could cry no more.

CHAPTER 16

EMORY WAITED outside the building a long time that day, wondering where Juliette was. She always came to meet him as soon as he arrived at the door. But not that Sunday.

He told himself, first, that she and Reuben must have gone to the market for some bread. Perhaps they'd had a hungry week. The thought made his stomach tie itself in knots. But the longer he waited, with a cool summery drizzle pattering on his cap, the more the fear began to build in his chest.

It was over an hour later that a thin woman, followed by a row of thin children like scruffy ducklings, came out of the door. She shut the door behind the last one, glanced at him, then glanced again.

"Oh." she said. "I nearly forgot. Are you Emory?"

He'd seen her come and go from the building a few times before. "Yes?"

"Juliette gave me a message for you," she said.

"She did?" Emory clutched her arm. "Is she all right?"

"She's just fine. I don't know what's happening, but she was glowing when she told me." The woman smiled. "She said to tell you that she won't see you today, but she'll tell you everything very soon. She thinks she's found Margie."

Emory gasped. "*Margie?*"

"Yes. That's all she said," said the woman. "Now I have to go."

He released her arm, and she hurried off with her bony little children. Emory stood outside the door for a long time after that, not knowing what to think.

※

REUBEN'S joyful tears had turned to snoring about half an hour into the drive. Juliette had never been in a carriage before, but she understood how he could sleep so soundly. It had a comfortable rocking motion, and the rhythm of the horses' hooves was so steady that it would have lulled her, too, if she hadn't been more afraid, excited, and hopeful than she could ever remember.

Reuben's head was propped on his arm, draped along the carriage window. His face was pale, Juliette noticed; though his cheeks were rounder these days, there were black shadows under his eyes.

"Poor lamb," said Ralph quietly. He hadn't talked much on the long journey. The pattering of rain had turned to silence, but the carriage curtains were still drawn. "I've heard that working for the rich folk can be brutal."

"It's better than working in a factory, sir," said Juliette.

"None of that now, Juliette." Ralph smiled. "Just call me Ralph."

Juliette returned the smile. She didn't think a grown man had ever been kind to her, except for Emory. "Thank you. Are we... is it much further?"

"Not much further at all." Ralph reached for the curtains and drew them back. "See. We're nearly there."

"Oh." Juliette gasped, loudly enough that she woke Reuben.

She clapped her hands to her mouth, and for the next few moments, neither of them spoke. They only stared.

Juliette had never seen so much colour all in one place before. There was hardly any grey here at all. Instead, green hills rolled to the horizon, streaked with the solid brown of wooden fences and the cool colour of stone walls. The sky was a dazzling pale blue, echoed in the ponds and streams that followed the curves of the little dales. Cattle grazed in the fields with deep golden coats. White sheep drifted over the green grass. Even the jaunty old farmer striding down the verge of the lane, his stick digging into the soft turf with every step, had a bright red neckerchief knotted at his throat. Its scarlet was echoed in the brightness of his cheeks, and he flashed a smile and raised a hand.

"Who's that?" Juliette asked.

"I don't know," said Ralph. "Never seen him before."

"But he waved at you," said Reuben.

"I noticed that nobody does that in the city. Strange, isn't it?" said Ralph.

Juliette wondered if they had been taken to another world.

They gaped at the beautiful landscape rolling past and rattled through a tiny village, no bigger than the market square where Juliette always bought bread. It was on the other side of the village that the carriage came to a halt.

Ralph stepped out and gave the coachman some money. "Come on." he said. "We're here."

"Go on, Juli," said Reuben.

Juliette was frozen to the spot. She felt as though she couldn't move, could hardly breathe. What if everything was about to fall apart the way it always did?

Ralph smiled at her. "Come on."

"I'm here with you," said Reuben.

Juliette fumbled for his hand and clutched it tightly, and they disembarked. The carriage drove away.

"Welcome to the farm," said Ralph.

The farmhouse that stood before them was old and cosy-looking and had no grandeur about it, but Juliette loved it from the moment she laid eyes upon it. Its whitewashed gables supported an old thatch roof that sagged in places but gleamed newly golden in others. The window frames and the shutters were painted a beautiful rich blue, and there were flowers blooming in the window-boxes, of which there were many. A few chickens pecked around the clean-swept yard between the house and the long, low barn. There was an elderly dog stretched out on the front step, its muzzle very grey. It opened opaque eyes as Ralph strode toward it and thumped a tail on the stone in greeting.

It was the quietest, softest, gentlest place that Juliette had ever known, and love bathed the very stones on which it stood.

"Come on," said Ralph. "She's been praying for weeks that she'd get to see you."

Hand-in-hand, Juliette and Reuben stumbled after him. They stepped over the sleepy dog and into a great old kitchen with a flagstone floor and a massive old oaken table that stood in front of a great, pot-bellied coal stone, on which a mound of bread was rising.

"Oh," gasped a voice that was wonderfully familiar.

Juliette's eyes stung with tears even before she turned and saw Margie standing in the doorway from the living room. It was as though all the world collapsed into this one shining moment, as though nothing existed except for Margie, her soft eyes wide. She was very thin, but there was a colour in her cheeks that Juliette had never seen there before, and the thin skin on the backs of her hands had lost its blue tinge. She wore a lovely, cotton dress, pale blue, that looked warm and substantial.

"Roo," Margie cried. "Juli. Come here."

She opened her arms wide, and neither Juliette nor her brother hesitated. They raced into Margie's arms and embraced her and kissed her cheeks and her hair, sobbing, clinging to her, crying out in wild joy. Juliette had thought she would never feel that soft caress on her hair or hear that gentle voice again in her life.

When their tears ebbed, Margie steered them all into a spacious but plain living room, with cream-coloured wallpaper and elderly furniture that was still more comfortable than anything Juliette had ever sat in. A stout old woman with a false scowl, judging by the loving sparkle in her eyes and the way she touched Margie's shoulder, came stamping in with a tray of tea and bread-and-butter. Juliette and Reuben wolfed down as much as they wanted—the old woman kept returning with more—and gulped sweet tea with sugar and milk. Real milk, fresh and rich, that hadn't even started to go sour yet.

"But how did this happen?" Juliette asked at last, swallowing down another gulp of tea.

Margie looked over at Ralph and smiled at him over the brim of her cup, eyes shining. "I think you'd be the best one to tell this story, Ralphie."

Ralph inclined his head. "You should be saving your strength anyway, dear. You heard the doctor—too much excitement isn't good for you."

"Oh, Ralphie, how can you say that?" Margie laughed, a full and genuine sound. "What could be better for me than to see my two little ones again?"

"Please, tell us," Reuben begged.

"All right, all right." Ralph set down his teacup. "Margie says that she told you what happened with our parents when she... when Bert took her away."

"Yes," said Juliette.

"Mama and Papa disowned her. I was furious. Now perhaps I think they may have done it thinking it would drive Margie back to them, but instead, it made them bitter. They were never the same after that. The years seemed double as hard on them, and last winter, I buried them both after they fell ill, one after the other. It seemed like a mercy," said Ralph. "They were so exhausted of this world. I was sad for them, but I knew that it meant I could finally do what I had longed to do for years." He looked at Margie. "I could go and get my baby sister."

"How did you know where to find her?" Reuben asked.

"Margie wrote to me just once, begging my forgiveness, when she and Bert had been married a couple of years. I was afraid to write back while my parents were still alive," said Ralph. "What if she answered, and our parents were angry? They were so bitter by then. But the letter had her address on it, and when I came to London to bring cattle to the auction, I went to her address. It took me to that ghastly tenement building where you lived."

"But we never saw you," said Reuben.

Juliette held her breath, a suspicion gathering in the pit of her belly.

"No, you didn't. I was too afraid to show myself to any of you." Ralph hung his head. "If I spoke to Margie, if I told her how angry our parents were... There was nothing I could do to help her, and I was ashamed. But I had to know that Margie was all right. So I followed her, and I saw her spending more and more time with the two of you. I thought perhaps you two were Bert's children from another woman, and I could tell how much Margie loved you. I started to follow you, too, to make sure that you were all right. I gave you coins sometimes when you begged." Ralph hung his head. "I wish I could have done more."

"Oh, Ralphie, you did all that you could," said Margie.

"You followed us," Juliette said. "Did... did you follow me to work?"

"Sometimes I did, to see how you were," said Ralph.

Juliette pressed her hands to her chest and felt the heavy thudding of her heart. All that time, all the fear she had felt... She had never been in danger. The red-eyed shadow that haunted her childhood nightmares had turned out to be her guardian angel.

"So you were the one who took Margie away last winter?" said Reuben.

"Yes. I hadn't seen her outside for months, and our parents had already died," said Ralph. "I wanted to bring her home, but I was waiting to see all three of you together, so that I could bring all of you home. But when I saw Juliette's face as she was leaving for work that morning, I knew something was wrong. So I went into the tenement and called Margie's name until I heard her answer. And when I saw her..." Ralph shivered.

"She was so sick," said Reuben.

"She was on the brink of death," said Ralph. "I had to move quickly. I wanted to bring you two, as well, but there was no time. I took her straight home, and for the next year, we fought for her life almost every day. She asked and asked after you, but I couldn't, I wouldn't, leave her side."

"You saved me, dear," said Margie.

"I thank God that I could help you, my baby sister." Ralph took her hand and squeezed it tightly. "I could never have forgiven myself if I had lost you."

"As soon as Ralph could leave me alone with dear Susan, he went to look for you," said Margie. "And so here we are."

"It's so wonderful to see you again, Margie," said Juliette. "And to see you looking so well, too."

Margie let out a deep belly laugh that Juliette had never heard from her before. "Oh, my poppet, you don't understand, do you?"

"Don't understand what?" asked Reuben.

"I didn't ask Ralph to bring you here for a visit," said Margie. "I asked him to bring you here to stay."

Reuben's jaw dropped. A delicious joy and pang of fear ran through Juliette simultaneously. She looked around the living room in wonderment. Could this be her home? Her own home?

"To stay *here*?" Reuben whispered. "Do you—do you really have lambs and puppies and foals?"

"We do, and we'll have more every spring." Ralph beamed. "That's why I need a farm hand to help me. A strapping boy like you would be very helpful, if you'd like to work with me, that is."

"Yes," said Reuben. "Yes, yes, yes, I would love to. I would love to." He was on his feet now, his face utterly transfixed with joy.

"And you, my sweet Juli." Margie reached over and rested a hand on Juliette's knee. "Dear old Susan is getting old. We could run the house together, you and I. But first, you needn't do a thing until the winter. You'll have the whole summer to rest with me and to feel whole again."

Tears filled Juliette's eyes. No more trudges to work in the dark and cold. No more struggling in the dusty factory, feeling her lungs draw tighter with every breath. To be here, with sweet Margie, in a warm house, to never see that terrible tenement again—it all seemed too wonderful to be true.

Except for one thing.

"Juliette," said Margie. "Sweetheart, why are you crying?"

"They're happy tears, Marge," said Ralph.

"There's something more." Margie tilted her head to one side. "What's the matter, poppet?"

"Oh, Margie, you've both been so wonderful," Juliette cried. "I don't want you to think I'm ungrateful. I'm so happy to be here—"

"But there's someone in London, isn't there?" said Margie, smiling. "Someone that you'll miss."

Juliette nodded, her tears flowing faster.

"Oh," said Ralph. "I see."

"Is it that lovely boy who used to sell trinkets on the street corner?" Margie asked. "Emory?"

"Yes," said Juliette. "He works at a factory now, and he thinks he'll get a promotion soon." She wiped her eyes. "You must think I'm a fool."

"Are you in love?" Margie asked.

Juliette's stomach flip-flopped. She thought of the way one smile from Emory could light up her world, of how he'd always held her in his heart, no matter what.

"Yes," she whispered. "We are."

"I am no one to judge true love, poppet," said Margie tenderly. "At least your love is for a good young man, kind and gentle, not like the monster I married. Still, my Juli poppet, you must know that I can never let you go back to that dreadful place."

"I don't want to go back there." Juliette clutched Margie's hand. "I want to stay with you."

"And you will," said Margie. She turned to Ralph. "My dear brother, I know I've asked so much of you, but may I ask another thing, for Juliette?"

"You may ask anything, anything," said Ralph. "There's nothing I won't do for you, Marge—or for this girl who kept you alive for so long." He smiled at Juliette.

"Then will you take Juliette back to London, next Sunday?" Margie asked. "Let her speak to Emory. Perhaps there's work for him in the village."

"I think the cobbler needs an assistant. Of course, I will," said Ralph.

But Juliette barely heard the final words. The joy, hope and excitement surging through her had been too much, and she fainted dead away in her chair.

CHAPTER 17

Aᴏᴛᴇʀ ᴀ ᴡᴇᴇᴋ in the blissful stillness of the countryside, Juliette wondered how she had ever heard the mad cacophony of London. The constant clattering of hooves and wheels, the shrieks of locomotives and ship's whistles, the chuff-chuff-chuffs of steam engines everywhere, the shouting, the footsteps, the clamour of bells, the cries of hawkers, the screams — it was overwhelming.

Even at this time of night, with darkness and smog hanging low over the city, the factory district still thudded and clanged. Juliette stayed close beside Ralph as they waited on the street corner outside the pottery factory. Even though she was wearing her new wool coat and her oilskin, she shivered.

"Are you cold, Juli?" Ralph asked tenderly.

"No, no. I'm just—" Juliette shivered. "I don't like being here."

The factory doors opened, and a flood of workers poured forth onto the streets. Their caps were pulled down low, their chins sunken, and each was scruffier than the next. The smell of baking pottery and unwashed humanity rolled over the street ahead of them, and Juliette's eyes searched the crowd eagerly.

"I'm glad I never have to see you in a group like this again, Juli," said Ralph. "I'm so sorry I let you work at that mill for so long. I—"

"There!" Juliette pointed. "There he is."

It broke her heart to see her Emory like this. He was among the throng of workers, head bowed, hat pulled over his forehead instead of sitting at its usual angle. He wasn't smiling.

Juliette stepped forward. "Emory."

He looked up. His eyes glossed over her body, then returned and lit on her face. Instantly, that smile she loved returned, along with joyous surprise in his soft eyes. He shoved through the crowd and rushed to her, grasping her hands.

"Juli, Juli," he cried. "Oh, I was so afraid."

"I'm sorry, Emory." Juliette embraced him despite the stench that rolled from his body. She had gotten used to being clean in the past week. "I wish I could have written to you."

"Don't be sorry." Emory pulled back, laid his hands on her shoulders, and gazed at her, his eyes shining. "Oh, Juli, you look so wonderful. What happened?"

Ralph withdrew to a discreet distance, and on that grimy street corner, Juliette told him everything. She stopped abruptly when she told him about the beautiful cottage and the hearty, country food, for Emory had covered his face with his hands, and his shoulders were shaking as though he was weeping.

"Emory?" she asked. "What's wrong?"

"Wrong?" Emory exclaimed, lowering his hands. "How could anything possibly be wrong? Juliette, you have a whole new life, a new fortune. All of my deepest prayers have come true." He laughed, his eyes shining. "You're safe now, and I— I will never forget you. I'll always be happy for you." More tears spilled over.

"Oh, Emory, do you think I'm saying goodbye?" Juliette asked.

Emory squeezed her arms. "If I can, I'll find a way to find you. But you must go, my love. You must live your wonderful new life and forget me."

"I could never forget you." Juliette drew herself closer to him. "You are the deepest love in my heart. I want you to come with us. Ralph thinks you'll be able to find work in the village. You could stay with us in the meantime."

Emory wrapped his arms around her. "Don't you want to forget everything about this place, including me?"

"No," said Juliette. "I would rather remember every horror than forget one moment of the time I've spent with you."

He pressed his forehead to hers. "Oh, Juli... Juli."

They stayed like that for a long time, simply holding one another, trembling slightly, before Juliette stepped back.

"So you'll come?" she asked.

"I will visit." Emory traced his thumb over her chin. "But first I have to stay here, my love, for a little while."

"Why?" Juliette burst out.

"Because the day I ask you to marry me, my darling, I want to know that I can provide for you with my own two hands," said Emory. "Whatever work there is for me in the village, I know it won't pay the same as the job I'm on the brink of securing. If I can become the manager of my floor, I'll be set." He pulled her closer. "*We'll* be set, if you'll have me."

Juliette cupped his face in her hands. "I don't care what I have as long as I have you."

"I know, but I care what you have," said Emory. "You shall have only the best I can give you."

Juliette closed her eyes, a single tear escaping down her cheek as she placed a brief, gentle kiss on his lips.

"Promise me," she said. "Promise you'll come."

Emory's arms tightened around her. "I promise."

EPILOGUE

IT WAS THE NEXT SUMMER, on a verdantly sunny day that smelled of apples, that Emory made good on his promise.

He had come twice to visit Juliette from the city, his train ticket paid for by Margie and Ralph. This time, he surprised them all.

Juliette was in the orchard with Margie and Bess, the curvaceous lass Ralph had been seeing for the past few months. Bess had a laugh that burst forth deep from the pit of her stomach and filled the air with love, and she was laughing now as she held the furious gander effortlessly, her arm encircling his fluffy fat body.

"Get them, girls," she boomed, and laughed louder.

Margie and Juliette scampered through the grass, trying to catch the little yellow goslings that scattered everywhere, peeping with great unhappiness. The goose, tucked under Bess's other arm, honked with great disgust as Margie and Juliette pursued the babies.

"Got you," Juliette cried, grabbing two goslings. She straightened up and turned to Margie, whose apron was already bursting with the other four goslings, nestled down and cosy.

"Silly goslings." Margie laughed. Her cheeks were flushed, and her shoulders filled her dress; she would need a new one soon, and she hadn't coughed in months. "You can't stay outside; it looks like storming this afternoon."

Juliette looked toward the west, where their rain usually came from. The fluffy white clouds that gathered on the horizon had dark blue bellies, filled with promise. It was so strange to think of the coming storm and feel no fear. It would bring water to the crops and life to the fields, and Juliette and Reuben would be safe and snug in the warm farmhouse, not freezing in the tenement as the damp seeped through the ceiling.

Emory had told Juliette, on his last visit in the spring, that the tenement building had been condemned and torn down. She was grateful to know it no longer existed.

"Looks like Roo and Ralphie have most of the sheep in, too," said Margie. She nodded toward the barn, where Reuben—

half a foot taller and swinging a shepherd's crook with ease—helped Ralph to shoo the last of the lambs into the barn.

"Hey," said Bess, "look over there. Is that someone coming up the lane toward us?"

Juliette looked. It was a strapping young man, riding a fat cob very badly. She didn't recognize him until he managed to stop the cob at the orchard fence and scrambled stiffly down.

"Oh!" She gasped. "It's Emory."

Margie and Bess exchanged a glance.

"Invite him in for tea, dear," said Margie, and they disappeared off to the barn, goose, gander, goslings, and all.

Juliette didn't understand. She waited in the deep grass, watching as Emory tied the cob, scrambled through the fence and strode toward her. What was he doing here? He had said he would only get to visit again in the autumn.

She wondered until he grew close enough that she saw the look in his eyes and the little iron ring in his hands. Then she knew.

JULIETTE SMILED as she took the envelope. "Thank you very much." She gave the postman a sixpence. "It's chilly today. Get yourself some hot soup."

"Thank you very much, ma'am." The postman touched his forelock and trotted away, clutching the sixpence like a prize.

Juliette closed the door of the flat and tugged her cardigan more snugly around her body, noticing how tight it had started to feel in the front. She hadn't noticed how cold it was until she'd opened the door for the postman. Here, in the flat, it was gloriously warm. When she stepped into the living room, Emory was on his knees, tucking a log into the fireplace. Flames roared, yellow and cheery, in the hearth. The cold wind beat against the windows, kept out by thick glass and lovely wine-coloured curtains that Margie had made, complementing the cream-coloured walls and the carpet.

"It's cold out today," said Juliette.

"Yes," said Emory. "We'll need to wrap up warm for church." He settled back into his favorite armchair. They'd scrounged it from a jumble sale in the village, but its leather had turned beautiful after some polishing.

Juliette perched on the settee, the one with warm cushions that Margie had made. "Oh, look, darling. It's a letter from Margie, Ralphie, and Roo."

Emory ran a finger over the moustache he'd been trying to grow since their wedding. "That's lovely, dear."

"Did you ask your boss for leave in the summer, to visit them?" Juliette asked.

"Oh, yes, I did. Sorry. I got home so late last night that I forgot to mention it." Emory extended his hands to the fire. "He was more than happy." His lip twitched. "I think the old man's taken quite a fancy to me, in fact."

"He certainly seems happy to see you when we run across him in town," said Juliette. "It's no wonder he made you the manager of the whole factory."

"He's a good man. I'm grateful for him." Emory leaned over and kissed her cheek. "But I'm far more grateful for you, my darling."

Juliette leaned into his kiss, then rested her head on his shoulder. "Ralph and Bess are going to have a lovely wedding. I can't wait to see it."

"Me, neither." Emory ran a hand over the slowly growing bulge in her belly. "But there's something else I'm even more excited for."

Juliette closed her eyes. She felt the warmth of the room, heard the tick of their cuckoo clock, felt the gentleness of her husband's touch, and heard the snap of the fire. Her unborn baby stirred in her womb, as though responding to the warm surge of joy and contentment that rushed through her.

"God works in strange ways," she murmured. "Life can be so difficult, so painful, so filled with loss. But sometimes, sometimes, even when life seems impossible..." She paused, remembering her dear mother. How she wished Beatrice could see her now, both her and Reuben. "You never know what might happen next. And sometimes, with God's blessing, everything truly does work out just fine."

Emory nodded at her, his smile warm and tender. "Yes, yes, it does. Especially with you by my side, my love."

The End

CONTINUE READING...

THANK you for reading **The Cotton Mill Orphan! Are you wondering what to read next?** Why not read **The Peddler's Widow? Here's a sneak peek for you:**

Daisy Parker rocked her child in her arms, gazing down at the eyes that were as grey as the sea. There was something mystical about those eyes, especially now. Sleepy and unfocused, they gazed vaguely up at Daisy, a whimsical smile lingering on the child's broad, thin-lipped mouth. It was Bart's mouth, but Daisy had no idea where her daughter had inherited those enchanting eyes. Bart's mother had had amber eyes, like him, God rest her precious soul. And Daisy had never known either of her parents, but her eyes were blue.

She kissed the smooth little forehead, velvet-soft against her lips, and rocked the baby in her arms for a few moments more as she sang the last few notes of the lullaby.

"And if that horse and cart turn around," she sang softly, "you'll still be the sweetest little babe in town."

Fannie's eyes fluttered closed, and Daisy went on rocking her, humming the lullaby's tune until the baby's breathing grew slow and deep with sleep. Slowly, she lowered Fannie into her small crib and tucked her blanket around her.

Straightening, Daisy paused for a moment to gaze out of the window overlooking the street below. It was raining softly outside, a thin mist of grey descending upon the brick buildings that towered on either side of the narrow street. Daisy could see little other than the wall opposite; like her own building, it was featureless but for small square windows at regular intervals.

But the building across the street had more boarded-up windows than glass ones, and Daisy could see small pieces of paper and fabric fluttering from the holes in the walls. The very sight was desolate, making her shudder to the core. She was relieved to turn away from the window and attend to the coal stove in the corner of the room. Her tenement wasn't much, it was true; there was only one room, and the lavatory was all the way downstairs and outside. This room consisted of a bucket for washing, a crib for the baby, a bed with a straw mattress for Bart and Daisy, and a tiny kitchen in the far corner. A large chest served as the pantry, and there was a table just big enough for the two of them, with a highchair for Fannie.

It wasn't much, as Bart constantly reminded her. But just as she constantly told him, after a childhood spent in the work-house, it was enough for Daisy.

She was cutting and peeling potatoes for dinner when she heard the familiar rumble of the handcart in the street outside, and her heart leaped with an even more familiar excitement. It was a little miraculous that she could pick out the sound of the handcart among the pandemonium of the city in the evening. There was such a rush of people moving along the street below that the sheer sound of their footsteps was already a cacophony; added to that was the rattle of cart wheels, the clop of hooves, the yelling of voices, the shrill clanging sound of a policeman's bell – but among all this, it was nothing for Daisy to identify that quiet rumbling. It was the sound she waited for all day, every day.

Click Here to Continue Reading!

https://www.ticahousepublishing.com/victorian-romance.html

THANKS FOR READING

If you **love Victorian Romance**, <u>**Click Here**</u>

https://victorian.subscribemenow.com/

to hear about all **New Faye Godwin Romance Releases! I will let you know as soon as they become available!**

Thank you, Friends! If you enjoyed ***The Cotton Mill Orphan,*** would you kindly take a couple minutes to leave a positive review on Amazon? It only takes a moment, and positive reviews truly make a difference. Thank you so much! I appreciate it!

Much love,

Faye Godwin

MORE FAYE GODWIN VICTORIAN ROMANCES!

We love rich, dramatic Victorian Romances and have a library of Faye Godwin titles just for you! (Remember that ALL of Faye's Victorian titles can be downloaded FREE with Kindle Unlimited!)

CLICK HERE to discover Faye's Complete Collection of Victorian Romance!

https://ticahousepublishing.com/victorian-romance.html

ABOUT THE AUTHOR

Faye Godwin has been fascinated with Victorian Romance since she was a teen. After reading every Victorian Romance in her public library, she decided to start writing them herself —which she's been doing ever since. Faye lives with her husband and young son in England. She loves to travel throughout her country, dreaming up new plots for her romances. She's delighted to join the Tica House Publishing family and looks forward to getting to know her readers.

contact@ticahousepublishing.com